BELOW GRADE

RECLAIMED HEARTS
BOOK 2

ELLE KEATON

MEMORY OF TREES

Trees are linked to neighboring trees by an underground network of fungi that resembles the neural networks in the human brain. - multiple sources

The woods were oddly muted that day. Even the crows and jays who always chatted and back-talked were still for once. It was a concentrated, heavy sort of quiet. The hush of many listening while others took turns speaking. If a human tried to eavesdrop —and most were oblivious to the voice of the forest—they would hear nothing.

A person would hear the wind, the soughing sound of branches rubbing against each other. Maybe the roar of the ocean not far away. But few would ever claim they'd heard the pines, firs, cedars, and hemlocks speaking.

A young crow with sleek black wings and a fuzzy head squawked and fluttered to the ground from its perch on an ancient nurse log. It was hunting the bugs that hid away underneath the bedding of pine needles and Oregon grape leaves. The winged creatures could only be quiet for so long.

This particular conversation had been going on for quite some time now, possibly for decades. But what is time to a thousand-year-old tree? A dark secret, hidden for too long, needed to be exposed. The time had come. Probably had come seasons ago, but exposing it meant great sacrifice. And in the end, the participants could only hope that the right two-legged came along so this concept called justice could be served.

What is justice to a thousand-year-old stand of timber? Perhaps not something the trees understood. But they knew *threat* and *pure malevolence*. It had walked among them for too long.

Far too long.

The backwoods have their own harsh justice. The unprepared, the weak, the foolish, they will be judged and found lacking. Even the prepared—the strong and the intelligent—can quickly run afoul of forest law. It might seem arbitrary to humans, but humans don't run this court.

There was only one way to get rid of the poison, and that was to expose the harm it had done so the humans could do their part. The young crow cawed and fluttered up to the lower branch of an ancient Douglas fir, as if it also agreed with the forest's decree.

Soon. Soon. Soon.

The rising wind riffled through branches and limbs, kissing each one and promising to do its part as it headed further inland. Underneath the forest, the soil—oversaturated from recent rainfall—released its grip on roots deep beneath the surface, roots that had held for centuries. A sort of sigh billowed from tree to tree, like ripples created by a rock tossed into still water.

Further underground, the secret waited impatiently for its turn. It wouldn't be long now.

MARTIN - SATURDAY

Fact: You can't throw a rock without hitting another rock.

Martin's move-in day was almost perfect.

The trip had been easy. They'd had to fight Seattle traffic to get out of the city, but it was pretty smooth after that—so, a typical day trip during a fall weekend when the UW played out of town.

It wasn't raining. The wind was mild. His closest friend, Simon Elliott, had offered to help him, and even if it meant Simon asking Martin if he was one hundred percent sure about moving every time they paused at a rest stop, the day was still basically flawless. Even if Charley, Simon's husband, who'd come along to "help," snorted every time Martin gave his simple answer of, "Yup." Even if his friends thought he was having a mid-life crisis, the day was almost perfect.

He couldn't have asked for more.

No, the imperfection—the complication—wasn't the actual moving, or the cabin he was moving into. It wasn't the life-changing choice he'd made to uproot himself and leave the city for the Washington coastline. It wasn't even that he'd spent almost every penny he had available to purchase a rundown motor-resort built in the 1950s.

As one does when they reach their midforties. Nothing to see there.

No, the issue was the ghost.

His attention slid away from the last few boxes stacked in the moving van to the marshy cattail-filled field and then toward the footbridge a couple hundred feet from where he stood.

The body of a local woman had been discovered underneath it only a few weeks ago; she'd been murdered and her remains had been dumped there like unwanted trash. An inconvenience.

A sense of unease rippled through Martin—not a feeling he was comfortable with. The homicides he was familiar with happened during binge watches of his favorite seasons of *Law and Order*. He was a fan of the original, but he also enjoyed *SVU*.

Technically, the wooden bridge that provided access over the wetlands to the long stretch of sandy beach that made this part of the state famous was part of his property, but locals had long used the path and Martin didn't want to be *that* asshole.

The murderer could literally be anyone.

Martin was a geology professor. Or he had been one until recently. He didn't believe in spirits or an afterlife. When a person died, they were gone forever. Scientific fact was the cornerstone of his life.

And yet.

And yet he couldn't shake the feeling that Lizzy Harlow's ghost was hanging around, waiting for someone to right the wrong done to her. The cops sure hadn't been able to do much. Cooper Springs had a tiny police force and no medical examiner or nearby lab to prioritize processing any evidence found.

It felt vaguely wrong. His new life was beginning where another's had been brutally cut short, and he didn't like it one bit.

"What the hell is that?" Charley asked, dragging Martin's

attention back to the truck and its contents. "Or rather, *who* the hell is that?"

Correction. Make that two issues. And the second was not a ghost. It was a red-blooded human man.

Reluctantly turning away from the back of the moving truck and his contemplation of the bridge, Martin peered in the direction Charley pointed. Martin knew exactly *who* that was. He'd just chosen to act as if the angry temporary resident of Cabin Five, the second fly in his otherwise perfect day, didn't exist.

Standing on the rise adjacent to the parking lot, silhouetted by the dreary November afternoon light, was Nicholas Waugh, Martin's short-term tenant. In his left hand, Waugh gripped a chainsaw. Martin could feel Waugh's stare rake over him, icy and unforgiving. This was a standoff, like Wyatt Earp and his posse, except it was Nicholas Waugh and his chainsaw.

Waugh's gaze was hidden behind safety glasses—to Martin, he looked like a disturbing beetle-like alien space invader—but those glasses were locked on Martin. Reaching down, Waugh jerked the power cord upward with a single powerful motion. The chainsaw started with a roar that echoed across Martin's property, even drowning out the sound of the ocean for a few seconds. Then, lifting his chin in a sort of acknowledgment or, more likely, a challenge, Waugh turned his back on the three of them and began attacking a stump, or log, or stump-log—was this terminology Martin needed to learn now?—that stood, if logs stood, in front of his cabin.

Martin suspected the living issue was going to make his life more difficult than the dead. Which, if he was going to be honest with himself, was a little depressing.

"That's the guy, huh?" Simon asked unnecessarily.

"Yep," Martin confirmed. "That's the guy."

"You sure he's stable?" Simon wondered. "He looks mighty handy with that saw."

Martin wasn't sure if Waugh was stable or not, but it wasn't as if he could do anything about it. Tenant law meant, barring criminal activity, Nicholas Waugh stayed through his lease. Bad chainsaw art wasn't considered criminal behavior, unfortunately. If that's what Waugh was doing. Seriously, what was he doing to that poor stump-log-whatever?

"Stable or not, he's got an agreement that runs through the end of August. My hands are tied. His residency was stipulated by the Davies estate as part of the sale."

"Huh." Simon moved to grab another box from the truck.

"Is that all you've got, Edward Scissorhands?" Charley yelled up at Waugh.

Martin chuckled. "He can't hear you over the saw. Regardless, I'd appreciate it if you don't antagonize him further. I do think he's harmless. From what Xavier told me, he's just a guy down on his luck."

"Said about every serial killer ever," Charley snarked as he grabbed a few more boxes that needed to go inside Martin's new home. "I'm down on my luck, so I'm gonna off a few dozen people."

"When you said they were fixer-uppers," Simon said later, "I didn't realize you meant rebuilding from the ground up."

Wiping the sweat off his forehead, Martin glanced around his cabin—not for the first time that day—and took in the disheveled state of it. The structure needed fresh paint, inside and out. New windows were called for. A new roof before long. The kitchen appliances were throwbacks to the 1970s, but they all worked. When his parents had remodeled their kitchen decades ago, Martin remembered the first thing his mom had gotten rid of was the mustard-yellow stove. The one standing in his kitchen made Martin a tad nostalgic.

The previous owner's children had left the owner's cabin as clean as they could. The work could be done while he got settled. He'd stayed in worse setups during summer digs in the Yukon. At least here he had a working toilet *and* a shower.

Besides, the geologist in him liked the idea of being able to look back through time in his own kitchen. There was something very satisfying about it.

"Fuck off," Martin replied without heat. "They *are* fixer-uppers. Quit channeling your inner Charley and take a closer look around you. These cabins were all built by hand, using local timber from the forest surrounding the town. Isn't that incredible? The doors on the kitchen cabinets were crafted from a single piece of wood. The parquet flooring is gorgeous. A true artisan designed them. All they need is a little TLC."

Maybe a lot of TLC, but who cared? This was his project now.

In addition to this larger structure, a cabin-slash-house, there were eleven smaller ones plus the "front office" where visitors would eventually be checking in. Once they were livable again, Martin planned on renting the cabins out to vacationers like the original owners had done. With the remodeling going on, he'd have to deal with Waugh at some point, probably sooner rather than later. The rest of the cabins weren't in nearly as good shape as the one Martin was making his home though, and he suspected there was more work to do than he hoped, but he'd cross that bridge when he came to it.

"TLC," repeated Charley. "Is that TNT loaded with C4?"

"You can also fuck off."

He would spend the winter fixing everything up and then he'd celebrate with a grand reopening of Cooper Springs Resort, hopefully before Memorial Day. Some people had affairs and bought fancy cars for their midlife crises. Martin had a heart attack, quit his job, and bought a run-down resort. And most people didn't have someone like his Aunt Heidi, who'd passed away last summer. Her last wish for Martin had been life-changing.

"Martian," she'd whispered, her voice close to giving out. He'd leaned in closer over her hospital bed in order to hear what she'd had to say. Martian had been her silly nickname for him all of his life. He'd always suspected she'd been disappointed he chose rocks instead of studying aliens at Area 51. "You need to live, *really live.*" Heidi had needed to stop for breath then, her lungs no longer able to do the work her body needed them to. "Don't keep wasting your life following the rules that mean nothing when you're dead. Don't die wishing you'd grabbed the golden ring when it had swung past you on the carousel."

Crying wasn't something Martin did often, and not because he was some alpha guy who couldn't lose control of emotions. When Heidi had passed only a few days later, he hadn't cried then either. Instead, he'd vowed to fulfill her wish for him. He would really live.

A week later, he'd notified the department he was retiring, effective immediately.

"Have you heard anything about the murder?" Simon asked quietly—as if Lizzy Harlow's murderer was lurking just around the corner, ready to pounce—bringing Martin back to the present.

"What? Oh, right." He'd been far from Cooper Springs. "No, they haven't arrested anyone," Martin replied. "The police think she was killed somewhere else and left at the bridge. That's what I know."

Martin had been considering replacing the bridge. Not that it would right the terrible wrong Lizzy Harlow had suffered, but it was in bad shape anyway, decrepit from years of exposure to the elements. And, it seemed to him, a fresh start might be in order. A new span maybe wouldn't remind Cooper Springs residents of a tragedy every time they crossed it. If it had been him left out there, he wouldn't want people to think about him being brutalized and murdered when they were heading to the beach; he'd rather be remembered for his life.

He set the final box, labeled *DVDs and cables,* down next to the small couch he'd purchased online. The couch was an odd shade of gold, but it fit perfectly in front of the living room window. He'd never be able to fall asleep on the thing while rewatching his favorite junk TV shows and catching up on other programs he'd missed, but he liked it.

"Last box," he said with satisfaction. Unloading the van hadn't taken as long as he'd thought it would; there was something good to be said about downsizing.

Charley plopped onto the couch with a thump and then sat forward. "Not too bad," he said before grabbing the DVD box and pulling it toward himself. He flipped the lid open. "What have we got here?" Reaching in, he pulled out Martin's box set of *The Bourne Identity.* "Matt Damon. Not bad, not bad." Setting those to one side, he picked out a couple more. "*Silence of the Lambs, American Psycho.* Martin, do you have a dark side you're hiding from us?"

"Like I would admit it to you if I did," Martin said, snatching the movies back and tossing them in the box.

Ignoring him, Charley dug further. "*Homicide, Law and Order, CSI.* Martin has a crime kink. But no porn. Sad."

"And all I can get you to watch are documentaries about vanishing species," Simon said. "Pot, kettle, the two meet again."

Straightening up, Martin's spine popped like a firecracker.

"How's the back, old man?" Simon teased, wincing while he rubbed the small of his own.

"There's a beer in my future and maybe an aspirin. And I'm only eight years older than you"—Martin shot Simon a glare—"and probably in better shape." Especially since the scare he'd had last spring. "Definitely in better shape."

He'd spotted the real estate listing while he'd been recuperating—in between bingeing true crime shows—and hadn't been able to get it out of his mind. The longer the property had sat on the market, the more Martin had felt it was waiting for him. Nothing like a cardiac event to get a person off their ass.

And the passing of his Aunt Heidi. He'd learned after her death that she'd left him the entirety of her estate. *"I see you fading away—just like I did. I don't want that for you, Martin."*

Heeding Heidi's last wishes, Martin had taken his inheritance, sold his house, and now… now, here he was. He almost couldn't believe he'd actually done it. Simon wasn't the only one who thought he'd made a terrible choice, leaving a tenured position at a major research university for a run-down resort. Frankly, there were days when Martin doubted his own sanity. He'd spent two decades working in a field that studied rocks, things that changed very little in a human lifespan. And Martin had gone and changed *everything* about his life. So, yeah, he worried in the dark of night that he'd made a reckless decision.

Yet here he was, moving forward instead of staying the same. And somehow, he knew Aunt Heidi was proud of him.

Raising one hand, Simon flipped him off and then winced. "Oh, that hurt."

"You need a hot pad? I have one around here somewhere." Martin looked around again at the stacks taking up the small space. There were boxes in all the rooms, and he had no idea where much of anything was. At least they'd gotten his bed set up first thing, so he didn't need to worry about where he was going to sleep.

"No." Simon glared at him. "I don't need a hot pad, *Dad*."

Charley's eyes widened. He eyed Martin in a way that had him crossing his arms over his chest.

"It never occurred to me before, Martin, but you do have that Daddy vibe," he said with a revolting leer. "All the boys in town will be flocking to you."

"Fuck off harder and farther, Charley," Martin growled. Stretching his back and arms again, he got a whiff of himself. He was going to need a shower before he unearthed his bed and collapsed onto it. But first, food. "I promised you guys drinks and dinner. Are you ready to check out the pub?"

The least he owed his friends was dinner and drinks. After arriving in town, the three of them had spent the morning making his new living quarters somewhat livable and the early afternoon transferring the boxes containing Martin's belongings from the moving truck into the cabin.

Charley batted his eyes. "Lead the way, Daddy."

Simon snickered. Martin glared and pushed him out the door.

NICK - THE ENEMY MOVES IN

Fact: There are 18 volcanoes in the United States that have the potential to erupt, all in Alaska, Hawaii, and the West Coast.

And then there's Nick Waugh.

Nick *hated* Martin Purdy. Of all the people in the world—*in the entire fucking world*—how was it possible that *Professor* Martin Purdy had been the person who'd swooped in and bought the resort?

Martin Fucking Purdy.

Nick had kept an eye on Purdy and his two friends most of the day, but he'd finally decided he needed a breather around midafternoon and made his way over to the Steam Donkey for some conversation. He'd been there about forty minutes when Purdy and crew waltzed in.

Because of course they did.

Nick refused to acknowledge them. Since the minute they'd arrived that morning, they'd been laughing and joking and generally being *happy*. Nick knew he should feel bad for not offering to lend a hand, but he just couldn't bring himself to do it.

He watched as they ordered drinks and food from Magnus and then chatted to each other—Christ, how much could they have left to talk about? The mirror in the backbar came in handy sometimes. The liquor bottles, baseball trophies, and stacks of glasses hindered his sightline a bit, but he still had a decent view of Purdy and his minions.

Damn.

Behind him, Purdy stretched and rolled his neck, his muscles tensing and tightening underneath his white t-shirt and Carhartt work jacket. Purdy had aged well, too well. Still spank-bank material. Maybe even better than he had been when Nick was twenty.

Definitely better. Unfortunately for Nick.

Professor Martin Purdy had evolved from an easy-on-the-eyes instructor to a hot silver fox. He kept himself in shape, probably working out regularly to be as fit as he looked. Nick would've remembered those massive biceps from the hours he'd sat through Purdy's lectures. They would've been etched in his brain, even if he hadn't been able to keep facts about sedimentary rocks straight in his head—those arms made him squirm in his seat. He also didn't remember Purdy wearing t-shirts so tight they should be illegal; could the man not find them in his size?

Earlier in the day, Purdy had shed his jacket as he and his friends unloaded the moving truck. Nick had stopped breathing for several heartbeats until his lungs reminded him he needed oxygen. Because holy. Fucking. Cow.

And the Prof was going to be living right here. In Cooper Springs. Just a couple hundred feet from Nick. He'd see him every fucking day; there was no way to avoid it without turning into a vampire and only leaving his cabin late at night.

Was this the universe rewarding him or punishing him? The

way Nick's life usually went, the needle was pointing toward punishment.

His attention drifted back to the three men sitting in the booth behind him. Purdy had his coat off again. Seriously, those arms should be illegal. Was it wrong that Nick planned on fantasizing about them later in the privacy of his bedroom? He deserved it. If Purdy was going to be in his face 24/7, he could also star in his fantasies.

Right.

So. No massive biceps had been in play back when Nick had been young and trying his hand at college. Mostly, his college memories consisted of the humiliating begging he'd resorted to when it finally dawned on him he might actually fail Geology 101. *No one failed Geo 101.* Geo 101 was nicknamed Rocks for Jocks for a reason—even the football players could easily pass the class.

Not Nick. Instead (after the begging), he'd been on the receiving end of a politely worded email suggesting he take an incomplete or drop the course because, with his quiz and midterm scores, he was unlikely to pass.

Below Grade.

He'd deleted the email, but it was burned into his memory.

Since he'd known exactly what his parents' response would be, Nick had gone to the bank the next morning and emptied his bank account. Cash in hand, he'd packed his bags and then driven all that he couldn't carry in a backpack back to Cooper Springs, where he stashed the stuff with his best friend, Liam. After which, he'd turned right back around and caught the next flight out of SeaTac to Southeast Asia. *Phnom Penh or Bust.*

It seemed like a good idea at the time.

And that was just in the first twenty-four hours.

"You seem extra gloomy tonight, son," Magnus commented, interrupting the unwelcome trip down memory lane. "Can I get you a beer? Or one of Forrest's lavender lemonades? I read that lavender is good for depression."

"First of all, I'm not your son, Magnus." Nick did not need Magnus's fucking cheerful crap right now. Not when he was hate-sex-fantasizing about the man who pounded the last nail into the coffin of Nick's college career. "And, for your information, I'm not depressed. I'm pissed off." And now, also, horny.

Magnus laughed at his words, which, yes, pissed Nick off even more.

His uptight, conservative parents never accepted any sort of failure. The Waughs had firm opinions about what success was, and their only child had never measured up. If parents could return children as defective, not up to standard? Yeah, Michael and Jerri Waugh would have been first in line. Nick hadn't spoken to them in eleven years.

Not long after leaving the States, he'd thought maybe they would want to know where in the world he was, so he'd managed to scrape up the courage up to call them. His mother had answered and before Nick could say much more than his name, she'd hung up. Failing out of school was just the excuse they'd needed to fully turn their backs on him.

He'd never tried to contact them again. Not even after he'd been injured.

"It's probably good for bad attitudes too," Magnus said once he was done chuckling at his stupid joke.

"Fine."

Magnus lifted one dark, bushy eyebrow, casting him a gimlet stare.

"Yes, Magnus, I'd love a lemonade," Nick said in a singsong voice.

Smiling even though Nick was being an ass, Magnus bent to open the undercounter fridge. Lifting out a heavy glass jug, he poured the pale-yellow liquid into a pint glass, dropped in a straw, and slid it across the counter in front of Nick.

Nick had to ask. "How come you have lavender lemonade when it's November?"

"I froze some this past summer. If Minute Maid can do it, so can I. What's got you scowling tonight?"

No way was he telling Magnus Ferguson—the second biggest mouth in Cooper Springs—exactly how he knew Martin Purdy. Or that his new landlord ticked all his boxes.

"New guy moved in today." He took a sip of the lemonade. It was delicious.

"Jeez, Nick. Be a good neighbor. We have new blood buying into Cooper Springs for the first time since 2007, don't scare them off. Think of it like *Field of Dreams*—build it and they will come."

Nick squinted at Magnus. "Have you been snacking on Forrest's special brownies again? And also, I'm pretty sure the guy isn't a vampire, so I don't know why you're talking about blood."

Instead of answering Nick—which either meant yes, Magnus had enjoyed a brownie, or he didn't think Nick's comment was worthy of a reply—Magnus's attention swung over Nick's shoulder.

"Evening, Liam."

"Magnus. Nick." Liam Wright pulled out the empty stool next to Nick and sat down, bumping Nick's shoulder companionably.

Arguably, Liam had saved Nick's life, and more than once. He was Nick's best friend, even if Nick didn't often feel like he was that good a friend to Liam.

Laughter rose above the other chatter in the pub. Nick glared into the mirror, trying to figure out who it was.

"What crawled up your butt?" Liam asked, interrupting Nick's surveillance. "This is a business you know, and," Liam added, poking him in the side, "sitting here glowering is bringing down the tone of the establishment."

"I'm not glowering."

Magnus was still lurking. He coughed unrealistically, and his fuzzy eyebrows shot up, almost touching his hairline.

"What do you call it, then?" Magnus wanted to know. "Staring into the mirror with a scowl on your face. If I were my grandmother, I'd tell you to be careful or your face would freeze that way. But," he continued, "I think it already has."

"Fuck off," Nick said mildly.

Magnus and Liam both put up with his moods, and Nick appreciated that about them. Magnus had even been the one to hook him up with the Davies estate. Before that, he'd been crashing on Liam's seventy-thousand-year-old couch. His parents had moved away from Cooper Springs when Nick left for college, so staying with them hadn't been an option, not that he would have asked them for a glass of water if he were dying of thirst.

He shot another glare into the mirror.

"Where's Garth?" Nick asked to distract Magnus.

"Had to go help out his sister. She lives in Ashland or some-where. It's the slow season anyway. Say," Magnus mused, narrowing his eyes first at Nick and then at Liam, "what are you doing Thursday?"

Nick groaned. He'd been so distracted he managed to forget the reason he'd been avoiding the pub recently.

"Nothing," he said firmly. "I don't celebrate the Thanks-giving holiday. You know how I feel about it."

An expression of extreme patience crossed Magnus's face.

"Nick. For Dad and me, it's not about the old traditions," Magnus reminded Nick for at least the tenth time in two weeks. "It's about the family we have and being together. In spite of your naturally prickly personality, Dad likes you and wants you to join. And, I suppose, I like you too, okay? You're a good person, Nick."

Nick released a sigh. Why was Magnus being nice? It peeved

him. He didn't want to like people. He *didn't* like most people, but Magnus, Rufus, and, of course, Liam had broken through Nick's defenses.

Liking people generally led to disappointment. It was difficult for Nick to trust; he'd been born this way, he knew, and his childhood probably hadn't helped. It took a lot for a person to earn his trust, and most folks seemed to not understand that he honestly just could not forgive and forget.

"No," he repeated.

Magnus smiled again, showing his teeth. "Fine. I'll just send Dad your way midday on Thursday, and *you* can explain to him why you're going to hole up in that drafty old cabin with no real kitchen and no real food, instead of hanging out with people who consider you family. You're not going to say no to an old man, are you? Besides, Liam will be here, won't you, son? I won't have to send Dad out after you, as well?"

Liam, The Traitor, nodded happily. That was Liam: happy. Always smiling. Nick should hate it, but he didn't.

"Yep, I'll be here. Looking forward to it," Liam confirmed.

Magnus's dad, Rufus, was in his midseventies and fit as a fifty-year-old, and he even had a girlfriend these days. Saying no to dinner would not be letting the guy down. Rufus's happiness did not depend on Nick attending the feast.

The "old" man was perfectly happy. He still spent the summers hiking the forest that surrounded the town, which was everywhere except for where Cooper Springs met the Pacific Ocean. He was head of the local Bigfoot Society. And even though he'd sold the pub to Magnus years ago, he still helped his son run it when they were busy or if Magnus had business that took him away from town.

"Yes, I will say *no* to Rufus," Nick insisted. The last thing he wanted to do was spend hours with a bunch of happy people, chatting and comparing lives. He shuddered. Sitting at the bar was different because he wasn't with them here; he was *near* them. He wasn't expected to interact when he sat at the bar. For fuck's sake, his *nice* shirt was a long-sleeved cotton t-shirt that had no stains. He'd picked it up in Colombo and somehow it hadn't been left behind when Nick had barely escaped with his life.

On Thursday, people would want to *talk* to him. They would want him to catch them up on his life, which—spoiler alert—was shit. He rubbed his jaw. Fuck, he'd even have to shave.

Magnus shook his head and grinned. "We'll be seeing you a bit after three, then." His attention flicked over to Liam. "Liam, it's always good to see you. You want an order of fries? And what can I get you to drink?"

Nick resisted grinding his teeth. For one, Liam was on the list of people Nick liked. And for two, he didn't have dental insurance. Or any insurance.

"I always want fries. Do you have that habanero-aioli?" Magnus grinned and nodded. "Cool. That too, please, and how about one of those stouts?"

Shrugging out of his parka, Liam draped it over the back of the tall barstool on his other side. Liam smelled like rain and saltwater. He'd either been walking on the beach or working in the carving studio he had set up in his front yard.

"Heya, Nico, how're things?" Liam asked him with a broad smile.

When he'd first crawled back to Cooper Springs, Nick had tried to keep Liam at arm's length. But it had been impossible. Liam Wright was the most genuine person Nick had known in his entire life, always truthful, but also *always* kind. Nick had never been able to hate him. The man was un-hateable even during Nick's worst moods. He just... ignored Nick's sharp bits and kept showing up in his life, happy to be friends and to do whatever.

More than once, Nick had thought it would be handy if they were attracted to each other. But the fact that they'd been friends since Nick's family moved to Cooper Springs when he was nine eclipsed any sort of physical attraction. Plus, Liam was just too fucking happy.

"Fine," mumbled Nick.

"*Fine*," Liam teased. "You don't sound fine."

"Well, Magnus just threatened me with his father." Truly, that should be enough, and Liam knew it, but he added, "And the new owner moved in today."

Liam understood him well enough to know which of those two things bothered him more. He bumped his knee against Nick's. "You knew it was going to happen."

Magnus set the pint of stout in front of Liam and wandered to the other end of the bar, where his dad sat working on a book of crossword puzzles.

"Yes, but why this guy?" Nick whined. He couldn't help it.

"What's wrong with him?" Liam asked. "I haven't met him yet."

There was nothing wrong with Purdy that Nick was willing to admit to Liam, even if they were best friends. No one in Cooper Springs, except Liam, was aware that Nick had flunked out of school or that said flunking had led to the vagabond life that had also recently ended in failure.

"I just don't like him," he said, knowing he sounded somewhat petulant.

"Okaaaay." Liam drew out the word, and Nick had the feeling the conversation wasn't over yet, merely delayed. "Are you working on anything new?"

Nick shook his head. "Nah. I'm kind of at an impasse."

Although he had taken his saw to an unsuspecting piece of lumber this morning just so he could see Purdy's reaction. Purdy had been exasperatingly calm.

Liam nodded sagely. "Open yourself up, and inspiration will come."

"How are your, um, princesses coming along?"

Recently, Liam had been inspired to create male princesses. He'd been gifted a mother lode of freshly cut pine and was slowly carving them—with his chainsaw, same as Nick—into works of art.

Unlike Nick, Liam had talent and knew what he was doing. The two carvings he'd finished so far were gorgeous male princesses, each over six feet tall. Nick was absurdly jealous of Liam's skill; the best he'd managed so far was a slightly pornographic dolphin. Chainsaw art was not easy.

"Great, great," Liam replied. "I'm pausing to decide who's next. Maybe I'll do something else first. I don't want to burn out on them. Besides, I'm gonna have to start looking for a real studio soon. The front yard is getting a bit crowded."

Nick nodded. Liam's yard did give the impression of a crowded train platform, albeit with inanimate objects. Still somewhat paying attention to Liam, Nick continued to surreptitiously watch Purdy and the two obviously younger-than-Martin men who'd helped him unload the truck. As he watched, they stood up from the booth and started putting their jackets on and moving toward the exit.

The door shut behind them. *Good riddance.*

While Nick nursed his lemonade, he and Liam chatted about nothing in particular and definitely avoided discussing Cooper Springs Resort's new owner. Nick stole a few of Liam's fries, avoiding the habanero sauce.

"I don't know how you can eat that stuff," he said, watching Liam smother his fries with the hot sauce.

Liam just laughed at him. "Wimp," he said, shoving a huge bite into his mouth.

"You are a scaggy monster." Horrified, Nick watched his friend continue to chow down his meal.

"A scaggy monster?" Liam asked around his bite. "What's that?"

"You. Someone who ruins perfectly good fries with mayonnaise and hot peppers. What the fuck is wrong with ketchup?"

Liam shrugged. "I like to change it up. Ketchup is just so… ketchup. Boring." Then he shoved another fry into his mouth.

Finishing off his lemonade and feeling antsy, Nick settled his tab, wincing as Magnus swiped his debit card. He needed to do something to bolster his bank account sooner rather than later. His laptop, and the last images he'd taken, languished in his cabin. Six months since the attack and he hadn't been able to do more than take them off his camera card. But he'd always have chainsaw art.

"I'll see you later," he said to Liam, patting him on the shoulder.

"Sure, take it easy, man. See ya Thursday."

How Liam could be so fucking laid-back when the world was going to hell, Nick had no clue. He'd asked him a few months ago. Liam had just stared at him for a bit and said, "I just don't see the point in getting worked up. People are fuckers, or they aren't. People are good, bad, or somewhere in between. I don't feel like I can change that. I can only control how I think and feel. Put myself out into the world and hope I make a difference."

Nick sort of wished he could be like that too, but that ridiculous notion was quickly eradicated when he stepped out the door and saw that Purdy and his friends were still there, talking and laughing. Tucking his hands into his pockets, he strode past them without acknowledging their existence.

Purdy called after him, offering a ride back to the cabins, but Nick pretended not to hear. Almost as if it was trying to match Nick's mood, the rain began to fall noticeably harder, and the wind picked up as well.

"Fucking great," Nick muttered, speeding up. The fat drops were falling quickly, soaking through his thin jacket.

He was going to be sopping wet when he got home. But the

day he'd accept a ride or any other kind of handout from Martin Purdy would be the day hell froze over and stayed that way.

Shivering and hunching deeper into his jacket—as if the thin material would somehow offer more protection if he made himself smaller—Nick kept walking. Halfway back to the cabins, an SUV slowed as it passed him by. Nick didn't look, didn't acknowledge anything, just kept walking. Martin Purdy could kiss his ass.

"Fuck!" he yelled, although no one could hear him.

His right foot and then his left—because momentum kept him moving forward—had splashed down into the middle of a kiddie-pool-sized puddle that had formed across the sidewalk. The muddy water soaked through the canvas of his Converse and socks, all the way up to his ankles.

He had no one to blame but himself. If he hadn't been a dick and instead accepted Purdy's offer, he would be dry and home already. But sadly, he HAD been a dick and now he had wet feet because of it. He growled, low in his throat, pissed off at himself.

Unfortunately, clammy feet did not stop him from dreaming about Martin Purdy that night. It hadn't been the first time Purdy had starred in his dreams, but it was the first time in years. And it was the first time since he'd been shot that he'd woken up with a throbbing hard-on.

"What the actual fuck?" Nick flipped the cover off his body and glared down at his dick. It looked back at him, happy and ready for a good ending.

What would it hurt? Purdy would never know, right? And frankly, knowing the plumbing still worked was vastly reassuring. Nick slid his hand down his stomach toward his cock. It was perfectly normal to jack off to the image of a man you insisted you hated.

Right.

He wrapped his fingers around himself, knowing already that

he was close to coming. The now fading dream had been vivid, but he'd startled awake just before crossing the finish line.

Arching into his own grip, Nick let his eyes fall shut and his imagination take over. Martin, naked, muscles straining as he pounded into Nick—nothing gentle. Nick didn't like gentle. Martin holding him down and making Nick take it. Nick wanted to take it, he wanted it all. His balls tightened and a spark of lightning shot up his spine and back to his dick.

"Fuck," Nick groaned. "Fuck, fuck, fuck."

God, it had been so long since he'd done this. Arching off the mattress as come pulsed onto his stomach and pooled there, Nick let out a roar and flopped back to stare at the ceiling.

This was not a good sign.

MARTIN

Fact: The heat of lightning striking the beach sand can melt the sand to form a glassy rock called "fulgurite."

"After you," Martin said, waving Charley and Simon ahead of him into the red brick building.

The Steam Donkey was Cooper Springs' only pub and its parking lot was about a third full today. November wasn't tourist season, not even day-trip season, so that was to be expected. Martin could have taken Simon and Charley to Pizza Mart, but he figured Charley would take one look and give that place, with its linoleum flooring and teenaged pizza cooks, a hard pass.

It was the Saturday before the Thanksgiving holiday, and Martin didn't have a good idea—or any idea, really—what to expect in his new town. In Seattle, the pending celebration meant everyone in the city ate their meals out in the days prior, filling the restaurants and making long lines at food trucks.

As he held the door for his friends, the ever-present wind buffeted against his back, as if trying to simultaneously tug the door from his grip and shut it at the same time. Martin held on to the doorknob tightly and, once inside, made sure the door was firmly closed.

The Donkey, as the locals called it, was maybe half full. Almost immediately Martin was too warm so he unzipped his Carhartt. Behind the bar stood a tall, broad-shouldered man who Martin thought was the owner, chatting with several patrons. One of them was Nick Waugh. Other diners and drinkers were scattered like salt and pepper across the rest of the space, and unidentifiable music played overhead. Possibly country, but Martin couldn't quite tell.

"Oh, look," Charley commented, not at all quietly, as he also removed his jacket. "It's our friend, Edward Scissorhands."

"Charley," Martin said warningly.

"Calling it like I see it. Although I think Edward was supposed to be nice. I might have to come up with something else."

"Do me a favor and don't bother."

Waugh had to have known they were there. From where he was standing, Martin could see their reflections in the mirror behind the bar. But Waugh didn't budge, didn't turn around, didn't make eye contact in the mirror; he refused to acknowledge them.

Martin rolled his eyes, sighing. What was he going to do about his surly, angry tenant? Maybe nothing. Another eight months to go on the lease agreement and then Martin would be free of him.

"There's a booth open." Simon pointed to the back of the pub.

Sure enough, in a far corner sat an empty booth, ready and waiting.

"Let's grab it."

The three of them crowded around the heavy wooden table, then Charley and Simon sat together across from Martin.

"This place has some atmosphere," Charley observed.

Simon frowned at his partner. "Be nice."

"I am being nice. I could've pointed out a lot of things, but instead I said it has atmosphere."

Simon rolled his eyes. "You use the word atmosphere the way your mother uses the word *interesting*. It always means she hates it."

Martin suppressed a laugh. The bar did have great atmosphere, what with the exposed brick walls, timbered ceiling, and old-style pendant lighting.

Charley's reply was forestalled by the arrival of the man who'd been behind the bar when they arrived.

"Gentlemen," he boomed, "thank you for coming in on this dark and windy November eve. My name is Magnus Ferguson, and I'm the owner of this fine establishment. What can I get you started with?"

Smiling and rising slightly, Martin held out his hand to Magnus. "I'm Martin Purdy, the new owner of the Cooper Springs cabins. These two are my friends, Simon and Charley. They helped me move my things in today."

Smiling broadly, Magnus shook his hand. Martin had half-expected him to play "who has the strongest grip," but Magnus didn't.

"Pleasant to meet you, Martin. It's quite a project you've taken on. Everyone in town is on pins and needles, waiting to see what you do with the resort. There's a lot of history around that place. My dad claims that Hollywood movie stars stayed there back in the day."

"C-list stars, if you ask me," Charley muttered.

"Hollywood stars?" Martin asked as Simon shushed his husband. "I wonder if there are pictures." Martin knew he sounded like a little kid, but Hollywood? This was exciting news.

Magnus shrugged. Obviously, he didn't think Hollywood was

as thrilling as Martin did. "There might be. If I were you, I'd ask Forrest Cooper. If there are any around, he'll know where they are."

"Forrest Cooper? Is he related to the town's founder?" Martin was eager to learn more about the history of Cooper Springs. "It would be cool to have reproductions of old photos and the like framed and hung up in the cabins. Give visitors a way to learn more about the town."

Magnus nodded in agreement; he was more excited about a local than Hollywood, for sure. "Yep. His great-great-grandfather, August Cooper, built the timber mill and the town to go along with it. He also built Cooper Mansion, but the family gave that to the city in the eighties. It's empty now," he added somewhat sadly. "But anyway, what can I bring you to drink? And are you hungry?"

Deep groans and nods indicated they were all famished and thirsty. Taking their orders, Magnus then headed back toward the bar. Martin suspected he'd be eating at the Donkey often enough while he brought the cabins up to snuff. Not only was the food great, but so was the conversation. He could hardly wait.

"Damn, this is it, Martin," said Simon with a small frown. "We're releasing you into the wild." He flopped against the back of the booth with a whump. "I can't believe you went through with the move. Honestly, I thought for sure you'd come back to the department. Aren't you going to miss Rocks for Jocks? The fresh undergrads? Their first finals week?"

His words were said with a smile, but Martin knew Simon was serious.

Martin shook his head. "Nope. I can't explain it, but when I first saw the property, I knew it was right for me. That Aunt Heidi was right about me doing something different with my life. I'll miss teaching a little, probably, but not enough to want to go back."

"You could have done something different in Seattle," Charley pointed out.

Martin shook his head. They'd been over this all before. "Nope, one heart attack was enough. This"—he tapped the toe of his boot against the wood floor of the pub to emphasize his point—"this is where I'm meant to be now. Everything feels *right.*"

It was difficult for Martin to put exactly how he felt into words. His soul was happy in a way it hadn't been in a long time. Not that he'd been actively unhappy, but he'd just been going through the motions, waiting to retire and die. Now he was living again.

"Even Mr. Pleasant over there?" Charley cocked his head toward the bar where Waugh was still sitting.

"Is this you trying to be nice?" Martin asked Charley with a snicker. Charley frowned and flipped him off. "Yes, even with Mr. Pleasant," Martin continued. "His lease is up at the end of August, so I'll be rid of him soon enough."

"Do you think you'll be able to rent any of the cabins out this summer?" Charley asked. "I bet the family would reserve a few of them."

Martin wasn't sure which horrified him more, the idea of not being able to rent the cabins out by summer, or having The Family come visit. Aside from the two men sitting across from him, *The Family* encompassed Charley's best friend Tobias and his partner, Arnie, and Duff—Arnie's friend—and his husband, Jacob De Rossi. The three couples and several of their siblings had all been adopted by Jacob's Italian grandparents, who were wonderful but, even in their eighties, a handful. If they did come to stay, Martin would have to take out special liability insurance just for them. They were like a family-friendly love-mafia.

"Maybe," he said weakly.

Grinning, Simon caught his eye and burst out laughing. Charley started to laugh as well and Martin knew he'd been had.

"Fuckers."

Magnus returned with beers for Simon and Martin and a glass of white wine for Charley.

"Don't tell Xavier," he said with a wink. "I raided his stash."

Charley took a sip and nodded his approval. "Someone around here has good taste."

"Xavier Stone is the agent who helped me with the purchase." Martin glanced up at Magus. "There isn't more than one Xavier in town, is there?"

A booming laugh escaped Magnus. "Would you believe he has an identical twin brother? His name is Maximillian, but he doesn't live in town, so no worries about getting them mixed up."

An hour or so later, his stomach full and muscles starting to ache, Martin was back outside in the parking lot, only saying goodbye to his friends this time. This part of the farewell had already gone on for ten minutes, and he was getting colder by the minute.

"It's not like I've moved to another country, Simon. You can come visit whenever you want."

Simon shook his head. "It's not the same without you. Faculty meetings are boring." He scrunched his eyebrows together and drew the corners of his mouth down, much like a toddler who wasn't getting his own way.

"I guess it's your turn to take someone under your wing. Search out that grad student or faculty member who's feeling a little lost."

Martin knew Simon loved teaching geology and was a dedicated researcher. Martin had liked everything about academia too—for over half his life—but he was done now and had no regrets about moving on.

"Right then," Charley interjected. "You're sure you won't come back for the holiday? The De Rossi spread will be fantastic."

De Rossi events were always fantastic, but that's not what Martin wanted.

"Thanks again, but no. I'm looking forward to just being here."

He didn't have the right words to explain to his friends exactly how he felt. But here, in Cooper Springs, was where he needed to be. If he was moving on, changing his life, it needed to happen in one fell swoop. He refused to spend his time driving back and forth between the coast and the city.

"It was worth a try," Simon said ruefully.

"You just want someone else with a healthy sense of self-preservation to join you," Martin teased. "*I* know better than to drink Paulo's grappa."

Jacob's grandparents had moved into a senior community, but the De Rossis were known for their holiday meals: too much food, too much wine, and non-stop laughter. The single time Martin had joined them for a meal, his stomach muscles had ached the next day—which was fine. The hangover had not been.

"Hey!" Charley protested. "I only go because Tobias goes."

"Lies." Martin shook his head. "Keep repeating it and maybe one of these days you'll convince me. The answer is still no. I'm staying here."

After several more manly slaps on the back and a bear hug from Simon, his friends *finally* climbed into Simon's Jeep and drove off toward Aberdeen. Martin watched the Jeep's taillights disappear in the distance as the first few soft drops of rain slapped against his cheeks. The end to his nearly perfect day.

Behind him, the pub door opened again, sending a beacon of

light across the gravel lot to illuminate the few cars left in the lot. He turned automatically to see who it was, which was silly. He was somewhere new, he reminded himself—he wouldn't know them.

A pair of stormy blue eyes met Martin's and Waugh's lips parted and slammed shut again without any sound passing across them. A surge of irritation rose in Martin's gut. What was Waugh's damn problem? Before Martin could confront him, Waugh turned away and strode toward the sidewalk, clearly intending to walk wherever he was going.

Over their heads, the clouds opened up and what had been a pitter-patter of light rain turned into a deluge. Against his better judgment, Martin called out, "Do you want a ride?"

Waugh didn't acknowledge Martin. He just kept moving away, his shoulders hunched against the rain, his stride purposeful. The temptation to tell him not to be an idiot was strong, but Martin resisted. If Waugh wanted to be a martyr, he was welcome to the title.

"He can be the King of Fucking Martyrs if he wants to. It's not my business," Martin grumbled as he climbed behind the wheel of his SUV.

Pulling out onto the main street, he turned back toward the cabins—*his cabins*—slowing down as he passed by Nick Waugh. The man pointedly looked the other direction, so Martin kept going. Fifteen minutes after he'd returned to his new home, Martin stood at the window watching his "tenant" trudge up the drive, looking very much like an angry, wet cat.

MARTIN

Fact: Making cookies is very similar to making rocks. The building blocks of rocks (and cookies) are various minerals. These ingredients can be mixed together to produce a variety of rocks. Just like cookies, some rocks are hard and some crumble at a touch.

Nick Waugh skulked around the property, but Martin didn't catch more than an occasional glimpse of his lodger over the next couple of days. It was much like having a feral cat lurking around, except Nick didn't want any handouts Martin had to offer. He heard the man, though, gunning his chainsaw like the thing was a race car from the direction of Cabin Five when Martin was working outside. There was also a great deal of profanity, as if Nick thought the word fuck might be going out of fashion and he needed to make use of it before it was gone. But he only spotted Nick once or maybe twice out his windows —with his trusty baseball bat swinging by his side—stalking the property while Martin worked inside.

It hadn't rained yet this morning and the scent of sawdust

and woodchips from Nick's creations floated on the air. Martin was curious about what Waugh was up to, but he had enough to do without playing at Lord of the Manor. Besides, since Waugh hated him on sight, there was no point in attempting to engage with him.

There seemed to be quite a bit of chainsaw art around town, some of it quite impressive. Who knew? Maybe Waugh was talented and his art could be displayed when it was finished. Support a local artist kind of thing. But as curious as Martin was about Nicholas Waugh, he wasn't going to be egged into some kind of weird battle of wills with him. If Nick felt the need to patrol with a baseball bat, Martin wasn't going to stop him.

A few locals stopped by, either to spy on what Martin was doing or welcome him to town. Maybe both. He wondered when —or if—he'd start thinking of himself as a local, too. Martin would never admit it to Simon, never even say the words aloud, but he had doubts about his decision to quit his job, sell his house, and change the course of the rest of his life.

Of course he did. But he'd gone too far to turn back now, so forward it was.

Last night, though, Lizzy Harlow invaded his sleep. He'd never met the woman when she was alive and had only seen one out-of-focus picture online, yet he'd dreamed about her. He'd known it was her in that weird dream-like way. The dream hadn't been frightening, but it had been spooky. Dream-Martin had been wandering around the haunted marsh like Frodo Baggins. He hadn't seen any dead bodies, but he could feel Lizzy's spirit. Beckoning or begging him, he hadn't been sure.

And then he'd woken up, which was a fucking relief. Martin had never thought he had a vivid imagination; creativity wasn't exactly a requirement for a geology professor. Maybe the upheaval he'd brought about in his life had knocked something loose? Something that had been dormant? Whatever it was, he wasn't sure he liked it.

That first night, after he got back from the pub, he'd hopped online to search for information about the murder. He'd found a single article on Lizzy's death, published just a few days after her death. She'd left two kids and a husband behind. The husband was in the military and the article stated that he'd been overseas when she was killed.

A few townspeople had agreed to be interviewed. Reading between the lines, it seemed to Martin to be a case of *if you don't have anything nice to say, don't say anything at all*. Although those interviewed did heap praise on her teenaged son and middle-school-aged daughter. And, it was noted, Wanda Stone had started a fund for the kids, giving a website address where a person could donate. Martin clicked and added to the fund; it was the least he could do.

Martin sighed and sank back against the couch cushion. He needed to do something other than obsess over the untimely death of someone he'd never known. He'd watch TV, but he hadn't gotten around to hanging the flat screen he'd bought as a moving-housewarming present to himself. Watching a show with it leaning up against the wall just wasn't the same, and it made his neck hurt thinking about it. Shutting the laptop lid, he grabbed his cell phone and jacket and headed outside. There was a chance cell service was working.

Simon greeted him with a "Hey, stranger!" when he picked up Martin's call. "Are you ready to return to civilization?"

"Simon, it's Monday. You were just here Saturday. Cooper Springs isn't the end of the world. You've been in more remote places doing research," Martin reminded him. "You've been to Antarctica, for crying out loud."

"Yes… but I never planned on *staying* there."

Martin stood outside his front door, under the eaves and out of the mist. His gaze snagged on the footbridge and the odd feeling of unease returned. Above him, a young crow swooped and sailed overhead, not seeming to have a destination in mind and not minding the weather. The corvid's wings were entirely unfurled as it floated up and down on the current, enjoying the ride. Martin could relate to that sense of freedom. He'd put himself at the mercy of a capricious wind and now he was waiting to find out what would happen, where it would take him. It was too late to turn back now.

"No, I am not ready to give up. Jeez." Even if he had just been thinking that it was too late to change his mind. "I'm just calling to let you know I haven't been kidnapped or heard any eerie banjo music warning me of trouble to come."

"They don't play the banjo over where you are," Simon insisted. "It would be the sound of chainsaws like—like a swarm of killer bees wearing hockey masks, coming to get you."

Martin laughed and rolled his eyes even though Simon couldn't see him.

"It's all good, no chainsaw-wielding gangs either." A fat drop of rain hit him square in the nose. "Probably those gangs are only around in the summer when it's not pissing down all the time."

"Speaking of chainsaws, how's your tenant?" Simon asked.

"He's fine." Martin peered toward Cabin Five. "He's been working on… something. I'm not sure what it is."

From where he was standing, Martin could only see the stump. It hadn't taken shape yet. At any rate, not a shape Martin recognized.

"Free-form chainsaw art, it's the newest trend. Maybe he's making a carving of you, Martin. A geology professor in wood." For some reason, Simon thought this was hilarious, and Martin was forced to listen to him chuckle for several moments.

"Right," Martin said dryly. "If you're finished? I was only calling to say hi, as I promised I would." He rolled his eyes.

"And to let you know things are going fine." And if he felt a little lonely, and adrift, and wanted to hear a friendly voice, he wasn't admitting it. Not yet.

"It's a plus that your tenant hasn't cut you up into tiny pieces and made a pie."

"That too."

"So you're positive you won't come to ours for the holidays?" Simon asked.

Martin shook his head out of habit. "Nope, I'm spending them here. What's the point of moving here if I leave all the time? And I'm going to spend Christmas reading a book in front of the fireplace. Maybe I'll even have a fire in it. If I'm lucky, there'll be a good storm. I can hardly wait." Martin wasn't lying about wanting a storm; they were different out on the coast. Intense and invigorating and, once over, they always left him feeling refreshed in—if he hadn't been a hardened geologist—an almost spiritual way.

"Okay, I'll quit asking. Charley wants to head that way after New Year's, so we'll see you soonish."

Were they planning on staying over in Cooper Springs? Simon was a seasoned outdoors person, but Charley was an entirely different matter. Charley's idea of roughing it was limited access to the internet and a wood fireplace instead of gas. On the other hand, Martin could take them on a chainsaw art tour of Cooper Springs. Charley was a museum curator. Surely, he'd have some pithy observations to make. It might just be worth it.

"Whatever floats your boat. We can have dinner at the pub again. It's possible a few of the cabins will be ready, but don't count on it. Although I don't think Charley is ready for even this level of the simple life."

"I'm going to tell him you said that."

"Go right ahead."

They said their goodbyes and Martin clicked off. His cheeks hurt from smiling like a weirdo, but he *was* happy. Even with the rain pissing down 24/7 and the wind blowing, Martin Purdy was as happy as he'd ever been in his life.

NICK

Fact: Sonorous rocks resonate like a bell when struck. These chime or ring-like sounds come from geological phenomena known as ringing rocks.

Purdy made no effort to talk to Nick.

That was good, Nick told himself. Very good. Excellent, even. It was exactly what he wanted.

Nick didn't want to talk to Purdy, either. But Purdy not dropping by to say hi so Nick could tell him to fuck off made him irrationally angry. The man could at least acknowledge Nick's existence. Yes, he realized he was the definition of ridiculous. Maybe *conflicted* was the better word. Wanting and *not* wanting the same thing with equal passion was the ultimate paradox.

Worse than Purdy's fucking silence was Nick's fucking reawakened libido. His dick had decided to acknowledge Purdy's proximity, whether Nick wanted it to or not. He'd woken up with morning wood every day since the man moved in. And, apparently, caving once to a quickie meant caving again. And again. At this rate, his dick was going to be rubbed raw and he'd end up needing a dick transplant.

The only solution was not to sleep, and that never went well for him.

Unslaked lust was the reason Nick found himself on the beach just as the sun crept over the forest and the bluff. The sun's murky rays glanced off the piles of driftwood and beach logs the ocean had haphazardly left behind as it retreated, and the now distant waves lapped against the long stretch of sand.

This morning he'd told his dick to fuck off. Instead of rubbing one out, he'd gotten out of bed, dragged some clothes on, and made a cup of coffee to bring with him to the beach. He was going to sit on the beach log and watch the ocean until his dick got the message: *No more Martin Purdy.*

Or until he froze to death.

Even where he was sitting, tucked in the lee of a sort of windbreak created by the bluff, Nick was cold as fuck. But he didn't have a hard-on anymore, so there was that.

The ocean had always been a calming place for Nick, even on freezing, stormy days. Maybe even more on those days. Way out on the horizon, dark clouds were gathering, readying themselves for another assault on the Pacific Northwest.

Lifting his go-cup in salute to them, Nick took a sip of the steaming coffee and enjoyed the path of warmth it forged through his chest. The random chirp of a bird came from somewhere behind him. Surprised, he twisted around to see what kind it was. Since the morning was chilly, Nick was amazed anything was up and about. Early birds did not get worms if the worms were frozen.

There was nothing.

Peering around and not spotting anything—not a single seagull or sandpiper—he heard the sound again. It was quieter this time. A weak chirp. A cheep? What the hell was he hearing? A swell of waves crashed against the shore and pulled back again. In the lull before the next set, Nick heard the sound again.

It was a mew. A very weak mew.

"What the ever-loving fuck?"

Dropping his coffee cup onto the sand, a sacrifice if he'd ever made one in his life, Nick began searching for the source. Whatever was making the pathetic sound couldn't be too far from where he'd been sitting, or he would never have heard it.

It took a few minutes, and a few more sets of lulls between the waves crashing against the sand, but Nick finally pinpointed the sound as coming from just a few feet away from where he sat. It was somewhere near or underneath a massive beach log that had rolled up out of the deep years ago during "the storm of the century." The tree had to have been ancient before it fell because what remained of the root ball was as wide as Nick was tall. The roots twisted into writhing curves, reminding Nick of Medusa's snakes.

Getting down onto his hands and knees, Nick peered underneath where the dead roots had dug into the sand. A pair of glittery eyes stared back at him.

"Hey, little one. What are you doing out here in the cold?" Nick whispered. "I'm gonna help you, don't worry."

The little beast fluffed itself and hissed, revealing a set of very sharp, pointy, white teeth.

"Come here." Nick held his hand out.

Hissing again, the kitten took a swipe at his fingers and retreated as far as it could into the shadows.

"Look," Nick explained. "I can't help if you keep trying to maim me. And seriously," he continued, as if the kitten understood what he was saying, "why would you meow and then not want me to give you a hand? If you stay out here, things could get bad."

The eye he could still see stared back at him, all but screaming distrust. Nick sat back on his heels, running his hand across the top if his head. What would Steve Irwin do? The damp sand was almost icy, the chill seeping into his knees and quickly cooling down the rest of him, making his thigh ache. If he was cold, the kitten had to be… really cold.

He bent down again and peered into the cave-like space under the tree. "Okay, here's the thing. You can't stay out here."

The kitten stared at him.

Nick stared back at it.

The little beast opened its maw and hissed.

"You're going to make this difficult, aren't you?"

Taking a fortifying breath, Nick lay down on his stomach—on the fucking cold sand—and bravely stuck his arm into the cave as far back as possible. He waved his fingers, fishing around for the kitten, since he couldn't see what he was doing at all. This was all by feel. And, thank-you-very-much, a bite.

"Gotcha!" he whispered when his hand brushed against its soft fur. Folding his fingers around the small body, he gingerly pulled the kitten out from under the log, managing to knock a handful of sand into his face and mouth in the process.

"Fuck, that's disgusting." Sitting up, he wiped his face with his free hand.

The kitten hissed and flailed as it struggled to escape Nick's grip, but he had a good hold. He, or she, wasn't going anywhere.

"And just where do you think you're gonna go, huh? A big old mean bird is gonna come along and swoop you up and then you'll really be in trouble."

Nick awkwardly shrugged out of his coat before gently but swiftly wrapping the kitten up in it like a burrito. Just its outraged face peeked out.

"See, isn't that better?" He cradled his jacket against his chest, doing what he could to help it—and himself—warm up. Goose bumps formed across his exposed skin and he shivered.

Checking around, he spied the go-cup right where he'd dropped it. Once it was safe in hand, he started back toward his cabin, very much not thinking about what he thought he was doing rescuing a tiny kitten. There was no veterinarian in town

—a real shame—and somehow Nick didn't see himself taking the community transit bus with a kitten in his pocket.

After letting himself inside, Nick set the kitten down.

"Happy now?" he asked, watching it struggle out of his jacket while it meowed loudly, making sure Nick understood: *Not Happy*.

Nick was thankful his place was so small. There was nowhere for the beast to get lost. Once freed of his jacket, it tottered toward the kitchenette on its tiny little legs. Was it brown, or did it need a bath? It probably needed a bath, no matter what color its fur was. It was probably hungry, too. Crossing to the half-size fridge, Nick opened it and grabbed the container of milk.

"Kittens like cream, right?" He poured a small amount of the liquid into a saucer and set it on the floor. "Let's get some food in you and then a bath." He was going to have to take it to the shelter at some point. Nick could barely take care of himself. He absolutely couldn't keep a cat.

Kitten stumbled to the saucer and enthusiastically began to lap at the liquid. It was making another funny sound. Nick bent down to listen and realized it was purring and drinking at the same time.

"You're going to choke yourself," Nick informed it.

Kitten paid no attention, just continued to chug milk. While it was distracted, Nick filled the sink partway with warm water and grabbed a towel from the bathroom. When Kitten stopped for a breather, he snatched it up and dunked most of its tiny body in the water, gently cleaning the sand and grime off.

Surprisingly, Kitten didn't fight him. Its tiny engine hummed louder.

"Are you purring again? I think you're defective."

He gently scrubbed the dirt away, discovering fur that was dark orange with white stripes and white socks on three feet.

"Don't worry, I won't let you be saddled with a dumb name like Socks."

By the time he finished drying the ferocious animal, it had fallen asleep in his hands. He wrapped it up with a t-shirt and almost tucked it into the blankets on the couch but didn't. It probably needed body warmth, so he cradled it against his chest instead.

The landline sat on the windowsill next to his futon couch. Picking it up, he dialed Xavier Stone's number. He'd adopted a dog recently, so maybe he'd know what to do.

"Thanks for the ride," Nick said.

Wrapped up in another of his t-shirts, Kitten was tucked against Nick's chest. The box he'd been given to carry her in sat empty at Nick's feet. The vet tech had written *Kitten* in Sharpie across the top of the cardboard carrier.

"Not a problem," Xavier said, far too cheerfully for Nick's liking. "Lebowski and I were at loose ends anyway. School hasn't let out for the holiday, so Vincent's at work. And, as you saw, Lebowski enjoys the vet's office. The damn dog is a sucker for biscuits."

Olympic Animal Clinic happened to have had a cancellation and had been more than willing to check out the kitten. When they'd pulled into the parking lot, Xavier's dog, Lebowski, had pressed his nose against the passenger window, his tail whipping back and forth as he whined to get out. Nick and Kitten thought that sort of excitement was overkill.

"What do I owe you for gas?"

Flicking on the turn indicator, Xavier eyed him while waiting for a car coming the other way to pass.

"You don't owe me anything, Nick. I feel somewhat privileged that you called me to ask for help. Is Mercury in retrograde? Or does it work the other way? I can never keep the planets aligned."

Nick stared at him. The car passed by them, and Xavier turned into the resort parking lot.

"Did you just make a planet joke?" He was horrified.

"Was it good?"

"No, it was terrible."

"Ah, well, I guess I'll never make the career change to stand-up comedian."

Xavier pulled as close to Cabin Five as he could. "Seriously, I was glad to give you a ride. You and I, we're both new in town, but also not. We've got to stick together, bond and all that."

"Or not, and we can agree to never discuss this again. Ever."

Xavier's laugh filled the car and Lebowski added a quiet woof. Against his better judgment, Nick found himself chuckling. Not a lot, not loudly, just like a snicker.

"Glad to know the kitten is healthy," Xavier said. "Have you decided on a name yet?"

"I'm not keeping her." She squirmed in his grip and let out a loud mew of complaint at being kept prisoner.

"Sure," Xavier drawled. "That's what the stop at the pet store and all the cans of kitten food, a litter box, and a few toys were all about."

"Just until I find her a permanent home," Nick insisted. The vet had generously not charged Nick for the initial visit but had extracted a promise that he'd be back for her next set of shots. The tech had made the appointment right then, and Xavier had assured him he could give them a ride.

"Right. Okay, so in denial. That's cool. I totally understand denial."

Rolling his eyes, Nick quickly popped Kitten into the box and shut it before opening the car door. Then he grabbed the bag of stuff he'd bought at the pet store. For Christ's sake, he'd only bought a week's worth of food and two toys. Hardly anything.

"Thanks again," he said before shutting the door again and heading up the drive. Maybe he should think about a name— just while she was with him.

MARTIN

Fact: Rocks are just about the most solid substance on Earth. Amazingly, they are changing all the time—even mountains grow taller or shrink, we just don't always notice.

Martin *still* hadn't been kidnapped by a chainsaw-wielding motorcycle gang.

He was a little disappointed, but likely it was for the best.

As he stood by the kitchen table staring out the kitchen window at nothing, Martin ate a quick lunch. A slice of turkey slapped between two slices of bread. Not exciting, but his stomach stopped complaining.

With his hunger satisfied for the time being, he decided to finally investigate the contents of the rickety storage shed. Honestly, he'd rather go to the dentist or watch paint dry, but he hadn't decided on any colors yet, inside or out, and didn't need dental work, so neither of those were options.

Three full days in, and he was tired of unpacking boxes and not knowing where to put his stuff. The to-do list did not seem to be getting any shorter. The shed, however, made him wary.

Who knew what kind of creepy crawlies made their homes in there? He was about to find out.

Armed with a heavy ceramic coffee cup and the key he hoped worked on the padlock, Martin hitched up his jeans and headed back outside. Setting his coffee down, he eyed the lock. It was rusty and grimy from the sea air. He tugged at it; the thing held firm.

"Okay, here goes nothing."

Forcing the tiny gold-colored key into the rusty padlock, Martin sent a little prayer to the gods before twisting. Incredibly, the key turned and the lock popped. One sharp tug and the door opened with a howling screech.

"Sound effects, just what I needed."

Picking up his mug, Martin took a deep breath and took one step inside.

The interior was his personal nightmare. As grim as he'd imagined. Worse than grim. Macabre. Monstrous. Thick dusty cobwebs hung in the corners, festooned with nasty crawly things—or the remains of nasty crawly things, which were just as bad. Stacks of cardboard boxes had sort of melted into each other, oozing into something almost unrecognizable.

There were definitely going to be spiders.

The drafty structure's better days had probably been long before Martin was born. If he wanted to use it for storage, he'd have to drag out what had been abandoned inside and invest in some weatherproof crates. At the very least.

Taking a fortifying swig of coffee, he stepped farther inside, eyeing the contents of the shed with great suspicion. The dank darkness screamed, *Here there be spiders*. He was deep in problem-solving-mode—as in figuring out how to clean everything out without touching any of the boxes and wondering if lighting it on fire would be a legitimate solution—when he heard a light knock on the doorframe. Flinching, he lurched upward, the top of his head brushing against the shed's low ceiling.

"Fucking hell," he shrieked, brushing frantically at his head and praying no arachnids or their relatives had fallen into his hair. His heart pounding against his ribs, he turned to see who'd scared the crap out of him.

"Oh, uh, hi there. Sorry about that."

An older woman waited in the doorway. Her salt-and-pepper hair was pulled back into a practical ponytail, and she was smiling at him.

Not a serial killer. Someone perfectly harmless.

Had Lizzy Harlow's last thoughts been something like that? Had she thought she was safe wherever she was and with whoever she'd been with? And instead, the worst had happened. Pushing the dark thought aside, Martin faced his guest.

The visitor held a plate of what looked like cookies. This had to be Wanda Stone, Xavier's mother. Martin spotted the resemblance between her and his real estate agent once his heart stopped trying to leap out of his chest and crawl away.

"No worries," she greeted him cheerfully. "Sorry I scared you! I'm Wanda Stone. I stopped by to welcome you to Cooper Springs properly."

"No worries. I was lost in thought." He motioned over his shoulder to the stack of boxes and other, less-identifiable objects.

She nodded, smiling kindly. "Not regretting moving here already, I hope?"

"No, of course not," Martin assured her. "I love it here. Cooper Springs felt like home the moment I got out of the car to look at the property."

Wanda beamed even brighter, if possible, reminding Martin of Xavier's smile when he'd signed the papers. "We're all so glad you're here, Martin—can I call you Martin? Or do you prefer Professor Purdy?" As she spoke, she held the plate—protected with plastic wrap—out to him.

Having just taken a sip of coffee, Martin barely managed avoiding spewing the liquid all over his shirt at her question. "Martin, please," he rasped and coughed, wiping his mouth with the back of his hand before accepting the plate. "I left the professor stuff behind in Seattle."

"Well, Martin, my son speaks quite highly of you. I made these chocolate chip cookies this morning. I hope you aren't allergic to anything. Just in case, there aren't any nuts in them. Maybe you won't mind sharing a few with Nick? I do worry about that boy." She stepped back, shooting an assessing glance around the shed. "If you're looking for temporary storage, Rufus Ferguson has a couple trailers he rents to the drama club and things like that, he might have a spare. He's easy enough to find at the pub, or here. I'll just give you his number."

After scribbling a phone number on the back of a business card for the Cooper Springs Thrift Shop, Wanda departed, leaving Martin a bit bemused, holding a plate of homemade cookies and wondering if he wanted to share them with Nick Waugh.

Abandoning the shed for the time being, Martin took the plate with him into his cabin and set it down on the coffee table. He could decide later whether Nick Waugh deserved cookies.

Martin hadn't spoken to Nick since offering him a ride home on Saturday evening. He had watched him drive off that morning in a car that looked a lot like Xavier Stone's. The big clue, of course, had been Xavier himself behind the wheel. Nick had returned only an hour ago, carrying some kind of box, and scurried up the hill to his house. At which point, Martin decided he didn't need to be a nosy neighbor.

If he wanted to know, he'd ask Xavier. What a detective he was.

He'd only just talked himself into returning to the shed, and its dubious contents, when the crunch of gravel in the parking lot reached his ears.

"What is it, National Visit the New Guy Day?" he grumbled half-heartedly. "I'm never going to get anything done around here."

Peering back out through the doorway, he saw a dark blue Cooper Springs police cruiser had pulled in and parked by the check-in slash front office. The "office" was a tiny structure, hardly bigger than the shed—an eight-by-ten-foot box with a single parking spot in front and a slot in the door for visitors to return cabin keys.

Martin had met Andre Dear back when he'd first looked at the resort, but maybe it was a tradition for the police chief to greet newcomers when they officially arrived in town. Or maybe Dear had news about Lizzy's murder? His gut clenched.

"Good afternoon, Chief Dear," Martin said as he walked down the slope toward where the chief was exiting his cruiser. "How can I help you?" As he drew closer, Martin saw that the other man's expression was grim rather than welcoming. Maybe it *was* something about Lizzy Harlow.

Andre Dear was around Martin's age—midforties, give or take. The chief was also Martin's height but lean, like he'd been a runner all his life, not a weightlifter. His hair was mostly silver, also like Martin's. But where Martin's eyes were a pale green, the chief's eyes were icy gray. And why was he comparing himself to Chief Dear anyway?

"Mr. Purdy, I'm sorry to interrupt your afternoon."

Martin cringed inwardly. He was going to have a t-shirt made that said, *Call Me Martin.*

"Please, it's Martin. Otherwise, I'll be looking around for my father and he's been dead for years."

Dear's grim expression didn't change. Whatever had made the chief decide he needed to stop by was police business, not a personal welcome to Cooper Springs.

"Martin, then. Can you spare a minute?"

As tempting as it was, Martin didn't point out that he was

retired and literally had all the time in the world. With the exception of needing to get organized so he could start on the remodel. And possibly find a hobby that didn't involve obsessing about a local woman's murder.

"Of course. I'm just trying to decide how much crap I can fit in the storage shed. How can I help you?"

The chief sucked in a deep breath and blew it out again before speaking. "We're asking folks to keep an eye out for a missing teen. Blair Cruz is her name. She's sixteen, five foot three, one hundred and fifteen pounds, with dark, shoulder-length hair. Last seen wearing a blue rain parka and jeans. Her older brother, Levi Cruz, thinks she also had on a knit cap. Blair left for school Friday morning carrying a bag with school supplies and extra clothing for a sleepover."

"Damn." He shook his head. "I didn't get here with the moving van until Saturday, unfortunately, and I haven't seen anyone matching that description." Martin pointed his thumb behind him, toward the row of cabins. "You might ask Waugh? He seems to keep an eye out."

They both eyed Cabin Five warily. There seemed to be no sign of Waugh, but Martin figured he was around somewhere. Nick and his bat.

"How come you're just looking for her now?" Martin asked. By his calculation, it had been four days since her brother had seen her.

Dear sighed and glanced back at Martin. "A bad case of everyone thought she was somewhere else. Until yesterday evening, when the high school attendance office called Cruz to ask where she was and why she'd missed class. Apparently, Blair spent the weekend at a friend's house, and her brother didn't expect to see her until after school on Monday. But she wasn't at school yesterday, and her friend says Blair hadn't felt well and decided to go home Sunday afternoon instead of staying over till

Monday. Her brother didn't know anything until the school called him."

Answering a phone call, only to have it be someone with the worst news imaginable, made Martin's heart hurt for Blair's brother.

"God, that's awful. Her brother must be a wreck."

He'd been an only child himself, but he could imagine the pain of having a family member go missing, or worse. Levi Cruz must be out of his mind with worry.

"Cruz is beside himself, of course." Dear said, echoing his thoughts. His gaze flicked to the left, past Martin's shoulder. "Especially with Lizzy Harlow's death last month."

Turning, Martin gazed in the same direction. The footbridge was in plain view from where they were standing, as were the few remaining cellophane-wrapped bouquets that rustled in the ever-present wind. And the hint of her ghost.

"Anything new on that?" He figured there wasn't, but it didn't hurt to ask.

Dear shook his head. "Nope, nothing. Her husband is back now. I don't envy Corey Harlow, suddenly being a single parent as well as mourning his wife."

Together they stared out at the wilted, damaged flowers and now water-soaked teddy bear that kept vigil for Lizzy Harlow. Maybe he'd take some fresh flowers over when he had the chance, or plastic ones that could withstand the wind and rain.

"Yeah." Martin shrugged, wishing he could offer more. "But you know how it is. New guy, so not in any loops. But I'll let the station know if I see or hear anything."

Pulling his wallet out from a pocket in his bomber jacket, the chief opened it and plucked out a business card, holding it out to Martin. "This has my cell phone as well as the station's main line, so please, do call." He gave a rueful chuckle. "I'm a new guy too, not quite as shiny as you are, but I've only been chief since last February." He sighed, looking around to take in the property, the bluff, and the sliver of ocean beyond. "And here I thought semi-retiring to a small town would be good for my health."

The radio affixed to Dear's uniform crackled to life and he pressed the mic.

"Dear."

A woman's voice said urgently, "Chief, we have a situation."

"I'll be right there. I'm only a minute or so out."

"Over and out," said the disembodied voice.

Dear sighed again, the lines in his face becoming pronounced. "That could mean anything from new evidence in the Harlow case to a report of someone stealing a rowboat and then dumping it in the cemetery."

"Well, um, good luck?" What were the right words in a situation like this? Was there police etiquette?

Nodding, Dear turned to head back to his car. He looked very alone.

"Us new guys should band together," Martin called after him. "Let me know if you ever want to grab a beer and vent a little."

Did that sound weird?

Probably.

Definitely.

He rolled his eyes at himself.

Why the fuck was it so difficult to make friends after the age of twelve? Before then, a person could say something stupid and the other kids would just ignore it, instinctively knowing the important point was *can I sit at your lunch table.*

Thankfully, as Dear climbed back behind the wheel, he replied, "That sounds like a great idea. I need a social life."

Martin stood and watched as the chief drove off, heading south toward the station. He was tempted to text Simon and tell him he'd made a new friend. Then he dismissed the idea because Simon would just roll his eyes and say that if Martin hadn't moved, he wouldn't need to make new friends.

"What did *he* want?"

Martin pivoted to face Nick Waugh. "Jesus Christ, where did you come from?" Martin's heart and nerves were getting a workout today.

Waugh didn't answer. Instead, he just glared, waiting for Martin to answer his question.

"A girl is missing," Martin answered finally. "Nobody's seen or heard from her since Sunday afternoon, when she left a weekend sleepover. Local teenager, Blair Cruz. Do you know her?"

Waugh's eyebrows drew together as he stared in the direction that Chief Dear had driven.

"Nope. I barely know her brother, Levi. He's older than I am, closer to your age."

His tone made Martin feel ancient, as if he was in his eighties instead of his forties. Waugh wasn't *that* much younger than him, maybe midthirties. In gay-years, sure, Martin was past his prime, but he had no illusions that he'd meet a man in Cooper Springs—or ever—and he honestly didn't care.

"That seems like a big age gap between siblings," he remarked.

"Mm-hmm." Waugh shrugged. "I don't know anything about Levi's mother, but I do remember his dad married a woman a lot younger than him. Then she died in childbirth. That gave the town gossips shit to talk about for years."

Martin wondered if he should be celebrating the longest conversation he and Waugh had had to date, or if he should be worried that trauma and death were what they seemed to be bonding over.

"That's... that's tragic."

"Yeah." Waugh nodded. "Gets worse. Levi's dad was one of

the fishermen who drowned in a big storm. That happened right after I left for college."

Then, as if Waugh realized he'd *accidentally* been talking to his archenemy, he shot Martin a scowl and strode back toward his own cabin without so much as a goodbye nod.

Well, that solved Martin's dilemma about the cookies. Nick Waugh didn't deserve homemade treats. They were all his, even if they'd go straight to his gut.

Damn, he should've offered some to Andre Dear. The chief probably needed cookies today.

Putting Waugh, Dear, and the missing girl out of his mind for now, he returned to the dilapidated shed. It was the only building on the property that hadn't been thoroughly cleaned out before Martin took possession. Whether it had been an oversight or purposeful, Martin didn't know. But he was certain damn big spiders lived there, and he hated spiders.

Taking a steadying breath, he stepped inside again and tentatively peeled back the lid of one of the moldering boxes. He was immediately greeted by the sight of an eight-legged beast staring back at him. Its front legs were raised upward as if demanding a duel.

"Nope, not happening." He let the lid fall shut again. "You win. Whatever is in that box can wait until I find a really big broom. I'm going to go have some cookies."

MARTIN

Fact: Over four thousand minerals exist, but only 30 of them are available in abundance on earth.

Martin woke slowly, stretched, then rolled over onto his side to peer out the bedroom window closest to him. His king-sized bed was a little overkill in that it took up most of the bedroom, but it was damn comfortable. And it had cost a lot, so he wasn't just getting rid of it.

He couldn't see the ocean from the window, but he could hear it. The rhythmic pounding surf had lulled him into a mostly dreamless slumber each night so far, offering a kind of rest he hadn't known he'd needed. What dreams he had focused on Lizzy Harlow, his subconscious brain working overtime to solve a mystery he had no business (or skill, for that matter) involving himself in.

"I should adopt a pet," he muttered into the stillness. "Then maybe I wouldn't feel like I'm talking to myself all the time. A fish tank seems cruel right next to the ocean though. Maybe a cat."

Rolling onto his other side, he picked up his cell phone. It had been windier last night than it had been the first three nights, but it looked like he still had internet access.

Aside from losing a battle to invisible spiders yesterday and doing some organizing, he'd reached out to contractors and reconfirmed dates for things he couldn't, or wouldn't, do himself. He was antsy to get the remodel moving along, and while Martin was handy with a saw and nail gun, electricity was a whole different scary ball game.

He'd also driven to Aberdeen and back, picking up various supplies he couldn't get in town—groceries, for one. And paint chips from the hardware store. Of course, the thing he'd forgotten to buy was a damn big-ass broom. There was no way he would enter the shed again without a damn broom in hand.

There'd been a grocery store in Cooper Springs in the past, and a hardware store too. He'd driven past the empty buildings on the main road several times now. The grocery looked to have closed fairly recently, while the ghost of the word *Hardware* was still visible above a set of mullioned windows next to the thrift store. He wondered if Xavier Stone had plans for those buildings, too.

It would be nice not to have to travel to Aberdeen when all he needed was a big-ass spider-killing broom immediately.

Blinking the sleep out of his eyes, he realized the off-white shade of the clouds crowding the sky outside his window meant it was later than when he'd woken the past couple of mornings.

"Way past time to get your ass out of bed," he scolded himself. "It's time for coffee."

Once that was ready, he'd fill up his go-cup and bundle up for a wander down the beach. He'd bypass the footbridge, however, and slog through the marsh grass instead. The bouquets of flowers left at the bridge by town residents were more ragged every day. He assumed it was residents who'd left them, anyway. Each morning fewer and fewer of them remained, having fallen victim to the wind and possibly small animals.

Swinging his sleep-pant-covered legs out from under the covers, Martin snagged his ancient UW sweatshirt and pulled it on over his head before adding a pair of thick socks. Taking his phone with him, he headed to the kitchen.

Xavier Stone had insisted Martin needed a battery-operated clock because of power outages and, in fact, had given him one as a housewarming gift. The kitschy black cat clock with zirconium eyes and a swinging tail hung opposite the kitchen window. He liked it; this kitsch was the new Martin.

The clock agreed with his phone that it was past eight already. Maybe he didn't have time for a walk on the beach. He halted in front of his mini-espresso maker in its special place on the counter. Coffee was the elixir of life.

Of course I have time for the beach. This is my new life.

The wind *was* more intense than it had been the past few days. By the time he got back, Martin didn't feel like he'd taken a walk so much as he'd been steered down and back up the beach by gusts of wind. The waves seemed bigger than usual and crashed against the shore in a way that had Martin wary of getting too close to them. Even the few seabirds hungry enough to brave the weather were hunkered down on the sand, as if they'd decided waiting it out was the best plan.

He was the luckiest man in the world.

Even if the worst happened and, for some unknown reason, he never got the resort up and running the way he envisioned, Martin was living in his version of paradise. Aunt Heidi hadn't known what Martin wanted, but she'd known what he needed. Hell, he hadn't known until he'd set foot on the mossy gravel drive.

"Thank you, Heidi," he said. "Thank you for everything."

The seasons would change and once the warmer months arrived, visitors would make their way to the coast and possibly to Cooper Springs, but he was lucky enough to be here all year long, and his aunt had helped make it possible.

Martin was thinking about the generator that was being delivered that day—and not Nicholas Waugh—when he rounded the corner of his cabin. Protected from the buffeting wind, he glanced down the row of cabins toward where something odd caught his attention.

"What the hell is that?" he exclaimed as he dug in his pocket for his keys, his cold, stiff fingers protesting the movement.

Abandoning the promised warmth inside for the time being, he squinted in the direction of where Waugh lived, trying to figure out what the hell he was seeing. A tall, slender pole had been erected in front of Nick's place.

Martin cocked his head, peering harder as he moved closer.

"You have got to be kidding me," he said once he stood directly in front of the carving.

Four feet or so in height, it had a round bulbous top and a stem that flared at the bottom. Martin was looking at a carved penis. And, if he was any judge, not a very good one. If he'd been Waugh's art teacher, he'd have given it a C at best.

"Jesus Christ."

Being a man, and also a gay man, Martin had no issue with penises in general. He liked dick as much as any man. However, he did not appreciate Waugh carving and displaying them on Martin's property.

Irritation getting the better of him, he stomped away from the offending art to bang on Waugh's front door.

He was ready to raise his fist again when the door finally opened, and Nick stood in front of him, blinking against the light, his blond hair sticking up in all directions as if he'd only just woken up. For the briefest of seconds, the man's guard was down. There was no scowl or anger, just Nick Waugh looking young and a bit defenseless. Again, Martin had the thought that he knew Nick from somewhere. This was followed by a flare of something close to *want*. His cock actually twitched, forcing Martin to shift his stance.

Hell fucking no.

The instant he realized it was Martin who'd been pounding on his door, Waugh's expression changed and he pulled the door closed so only a sliver of his body showed. His light eyebrows drew together—*there was that familiar scowl*—and the sense of recognition vanished.

"What do you want?" Waugh demanded.

Martin was not an angry man; he prided himself on being calm and levelheaded. He was not going to let Waugh get to him.

"I want to know why you've decided to display a penis on my property."

Confusion and then something like amusement flickered across Waugh's face, replacing the glower for a quarter of a moment.

"Freedom of speech."

Martin was fairly certain freedom of speech had nothing to do with chainsaw-carved cocks. He sucked in a breath through his nose.

"Nope. Take it down or put it around back where it can't be seen from the road. If it's here at the end of the day, I'm throwing it on the fire pit and having a pleasant bonfire. Maybe I'll invite some local kids and have s'mores."

"Just you try," Nick snarled as he heaved the door shut.

Martin stared at the weatherworn door as it vibrated an inch from his nose.

That could have gone better. Maybe next time I should try that levelheadedness thing.

What he also needed to do was research tenant rights.

Another eight months of this was starting to feel like a very long time.

But the research never happened because the delivery van with the generator Martin had ordered a month ago arrived. It was soon followed by the electrician who was doing him a massive favor by hooking it up during the holiday week.

Out of the corner of his eye, Martin saw Nick's door open. He surreptitiously watched as the man exited and strode down the hill and toward the road without looking in Martin's direction. The stiffness in his shoulders told Martin that Nick had seen him and chose to ignore him and leave the penis carving right where it was.

Martin was sorely tempted to do something about the wooden phallus while Nick was out but decided against it. He would try having a calm, adult conversation with Waugh. *Then* he would do something about the cock.

Several hours later, Electrician Rob was wiping his hands off on an already greasy work towel. "This should hold you for now," Rob said. "But I recommend updating all the boxes as soon as you can. Glad I could get out here for you today."

Martin was freezing—the wind had picked up even more and the temperatures had dropped—but he'd felt like he needed to keep Rob company while he hooked the generator up. Pretty, the machine wasn't, but he'd enjoyed talking with Rob while he worked. In a power outage, the machine would automatically switch on and provide power to his cabin and the four closest to him.

The other seven would have to wait until he updated the electric boxes.

While he'd watched Rob work, Waugh's expression when he opened his door played over and over again on Martin's mental screen. For those fleeting seconds, Martin had thought maybe he recognized Nick. It had to be a figment of his imagination—along with his dick's reaction. But, for reasons only understood by his cock and balls, he couldn't stop rolling the thought and the nebulous *want* around in his brain.

He'd never go there. Nick Waugh was a porcupine mixed with a cactus and a smidgeon of pissed-off cat. And besides, Martin wasn't looking for anyone, partner or otherwise.

Shoving the last of his tools into his toolbox, Rob closed the lid with a snap.

"You have my card. Give me a call when you're ready to do the rest."

Promising to call after the beginning of the year, Martin walked Rob to his van, where they stopped to shake hands.

"Thanks again," he said before Rob drove off, heading toward Aberdeen.

Feeling at loose ends, even with boxes still to unpack and belongings he needed to find places for, Martin decided to stroll over to the Steam Donkey. One of these days he'd try the pizza place, but this early evening he wanted a beer and adult conversation.

He felt certain that publican Magnus Ferguson would provide both.

Martin was greeted with a booming, "Welcome, have a seat," when he pushed inside the pub. As usual, he was instantly too warm and began to peel off his layers. Maybe by next year he'd figure out how to dress properly for the shift in temperature between inside and outside.

Noting there was plenty of seating at the bar, the best spot for making conversation, he chose a seat at the end nearest to the door. He was two barstools away from an older man who, on a second glance, looked enough like Magnus that they had to be related.

"You must be Martin Purdy," the older man said. "Rufus Ferguson. Call me Rufus." He held out an aged and battered hand.

Shaking Rufus's hand, Martin agreed that, yes, he was Martin Purdy, the guy who'd bought Cooper Springs Resort.

"Nice to have some new blood in town," Rufus remarked. "I was starting to think Cooper Springs was going to dry up and blow away."

"It might blow away, Pops, but I don't think it will be dry when it happens." Magnus leaned an elbow on the bar. "What can I pour you?"

Martin perused the tap list and decided on an IPA called Screaming Trees, which he personally found hilarious, even if he wasn't a fan.

Returning with his beer, Magnus tossed a coaster on the counter and set the glass on it in front of Martin.

"So, how's it going? Everything moved in? Pops told me Rob was out this morning."

Ah, yes, the art of small-town communications. Martin had grown up in a small town, so he was familiar, even if it had been a while.

"Yep, doing good. Had a generator installed, seemed like a good idea. And have to admit, Xavier was the one who suggested it."

This devolved into a discussion about what brand Martin had chosen and how there were quieter generators, but they didn't put out as much power.

The door opened again and more townies trickled inside to take up a few more spots at the bar. Martin vaguely wondered where Nick was hiding or if he'd gone back to his cabin. A red-haired man about Martin's age, maybe a few years younger, took the stool next to him.

"You serving today or just talking people's ears off?" he asked Magnus.

"Are you taking correspondence classes in comedy school? They're not worth the money," Magnus quipped.

The guy started to laugh, making Martin smile along with him. "Old man, you do know about the internet? There's no such thing as correspondence school in this century."

"Feck off. What do you want to drink so I can ignore you the rest of the night?" Magnus looked at Martin and seemed to realize he had no idea who the man was. "Martin, my friend, this here is Forrest Cooper. Now you know who he is, you can cross to the other side of the street when you see him."

Turning in his seat, Forrest grinned at Martin. "You must be Martin Purdy, the savior of Cooper Springs." The tone was such that Martin knew he was teasing. Forrest stuck his hand out. "Forrest Cooper—yes, I'm related—but, instead of timber, I have a lavender farm north of town."

Martin shook his hand. "Martin Purdy. It's a pleasure to meet you."

"I can assure you, not many people have said that," Magnus interjected as he set Forrest's beer down and walked to the other end of the bar.

"True, old man," said Forrest, nodding morosely, "so why don't you let me have my time in the limelight?"

"A lavender farm?" Martin knew there were several large farms further south but hadn't realized Cooper Springs had one.

"It's a work in progress. I've been planting for several years, trying to find the best variety for the area and for the soil I have. Xavier thinks the farm will draw visitors to town. But of course, lavender only blooms in the summer months, so I'm not sure it falls in line with his master plan. I'm also perfecting small-batch lavender lemonade. Magnus has some on hand if you ever want a taste."

Martin thought Xavier was on to something. The more there was unique about Cooper Springs—like a lavender farm—the more people would want to come and stay for a while.

"Would it be possible for me to come out for a visit one of these days? The cabins aren't going to be ready for months, and that's if I'm lucky," he admitted, "but tourists love locally produced goods, right? Maybe I could source some lavender for bouquets and sachets?"

Martin wanted to start off on the right foot in Cooper Springs. He was here to begin a new life and make new connections, and it seemed like offering a way for locals to be a part of the rejuvenation of the resort was a good first step.

Forrest's broad grin grew wider. "Absolutely. I'd planned on stopping by and leaving some info for you anyway, but business over beers is better. You moved in this weekend, right? How's it going?" He leaned a little closer to Martin. "How's Nick?"

Martin wasn't one to gossip, but he must have hesitated a beat too long. Forrest reached out and patted his arm.

"Like that, huh? About what I figured. Nick's not a bad person. He's just been through a lot, and getting shot probably didn't help."

"Forrest," Magnus boomed.

Forrest snapped his mouth shut, giving Martin a semi-guilty look before spinning around to look at Magnus.

"Yes, my liege?"

"What're you bringing tomorrow?"

"Oh." Forrest's shoulders slumped as if he'd been expecting something more. "I was thinking a big batch of focaccia."

"Focaccia," Magnus mused. "That'll work. Pop's doing lamb and some curry recipe he wants to test on us. Critter is roasting a turkey. Wanda is doing two kinds of potatoes." His attention swung to Martin. "Are you coming?"

"Um, coming to what?"

"Ah, damn, I knew I'd forgotten something. It's our annual community celebration, my poor version of a Samhain feast—which, yes, I know is the end of October, but we can't close the pub that day. Tomorrow is the only day Pops and I close the pub to the public, and we invite our friends to eat with us."

"I'm not exactly a friend."

"Not yet, you aren't, but I can tell you will be. Probably you can't cook anything in that kitchen of yours yet, so don't worry about bringing anything. Everyone is going to want to get to know you anyway. Be here around three."

Someone called for Magnus and he marched off without waiting for Martin's reply. Martin wasn't sure if Magnus had been planning to wait anyway; the exchange felt more like an order than an invitation.

"I guess we'll be seeing you tomorrow, then," Forrest commented. "It's really for the best this way, like ripping off a Band-Aid. You'll get to meet most of us in one fell swoop."

Martin nodded, not really paying attention. Forrest said something about a king and the weather channel, but Martin couldn't care less. He was stuck on the comment about Nick Waugh.

He'd been shot? What were the circumstances? Martin wanted to know more. But the moment had passed, and it didn't feel right to force a return to it, even if he suspected Forrest Cooper would be more than happy to tell him. Because he also suspected Nick Waugh hated that people in town gossiped about him.

NICK

Fact: Antacids taste like chalk because they are calcium carbonate, which is… chalk.

Nick didn't sleep much the night he learned Blair Cruz was missing. Not that he ever slept deeply, but after hearing the news from Purdy, he physically wasn't able to close his eyes. Instead, he lay on the cabin's futon couch and watched the darkness while Kitten purred on his chest.

No one in town believed him when he'd mentioned that something—more likely *someone*—was making the back of his neck twitch. Worse, everyone sitting at the bar that night over a month ago had laughed. Magnus had clapped him on the shoulder—hard—saying something about Nick still being shaken from the ambush at a Sri Lankan market and seeing shadows at every corner. Even Liam thought Nick was overreacting. And that betrayal burned.

"Maybe try meditation. It helps me relax," Liam had suggested, nudging Nick with his elbow and doing his best to take the sting of the laughter away.

To that irritating proposal, Nick had replied, "Dude, if you were any more relaxed, you'd be a puddle." But he'd left it at that, not mentioning his "edgy feelings" again. If people chose not to believe him, that was on them.

And Magnus did have a point. Nick *was* still shaken by what had happened to him. He'd been fucking shot and had nearly died. All he'd wanted was a nice ripe mango and instead his life had changed forever.

But since that night at the Steam Donkey, Lizzy Harlow had been murdered and now Blair Cruz was missing.

To some extent, he probably did have a bad case of *what just went bump in the night*. Nick was willing to concede that much. He stroked Kitten's soft fur as she snuffled and turned around, making herself comfortable in his armpit.

But.

BUT.

Being jumpy didn't mean Nick was wrong about the shiny men-in-black-style SUVs he'd spotted driving through and around town at odd hours of the day and night. Or the supposed Sasquatch sightings that had increased from the usual numbers. Where there was smoke, there was fire, not wee fairies—or a large Bigfoot—dancing around in a mushroom circle.

The first time he'd seen a black SUV was back at the beginning of October, and he'd brushed it off as late-season tourists. The thing was, not many tourists who came to Cooper Springs drove that kind of vehicle.

Kitten shifted and stretched her body as long as she could. Nick ran his hand across her soft fur, not sure if he was calming her or himself.

Visitors were more likely to drive minivans full of kids, dogs, camping equipment, and kites. Or they drove vehicles with four-wheel drive, ones designed for the forest roads, and left them parked at trailheads. The sporty cars were usually day-trippers taking their little car for a spin along the rugged coast or driving them out onto the beach.

Nick didn't believe in Bigfoot, the Sasquatch, or the Yeti. He indulged Rufus Ferguson's natter about the mythical beasts but did not believe they existed. What *did* exist were bad humans. And bad humans who hid out in the timberland surrounding Cooper Springs were the worst kind of bad.

Forrest Cooper might understand Nick's point of view. Nick suspected he might. But he hadn't yet screwed up the courage to follow up with Forrest about the cars he'd seen or the supposed Bigfoot sightings this past summer. And he certainly wasn't going to the police about it.

Nick considered Forrest a friend of sorts—or, somewhat of an outcast like himself. They had beers at the Donkey and swapped tall tales, but one thing Forrest never talked about was his life—and his younger sister's life—before their grandfather rescued the siblings and brought them back to live with him. Forrest had his own reasons to believe what people thought were Bigfoot and his brethren were actually *humans,* and up to no good. Nick's relationship with his parents was nonexistent nowadays, but they'd at least done the basics and hadn't made him live in the woods and scrounge for food to survive.

Humanity was the most frightening monster of all.

The night of Lizzy Harlow's murder, Nick hadn't seen—or heard—anything out of the ordinary or even ordinary. He hadn't liked her, hadn't even known her that well. He didn't think many in town had. But she certainly didn't deserve her fate, and Nick had this nagging feeling he'd let her down somehow. He should have been watching. He knew—because information was currency in a small town—that she hadn't been killed at the bridge. Some murdering creep *murdered* her and then brought her body to the marsh, where it had been discovered by Xavier Stone and Vincent Barone.

In Nick's opinion, that could mean one of several things.

One, the killer *wanted* the body to be found and knew the footpath to the beach was popular—thus, they were local. Two, they'd thought the bridge was as good a place as any to dump her—could be local, could be from out of town. Although an out-of-towner was less likely to know about the footpath. And last, the killer didn't know that the bridge and path were used regularly, even in the foulest weather, and had thought they stumbled upon a good place to hide the body—therefore, from out of town.

All Nick knew for certain was that he felt he'd failed Lizzy Harlow. He should've have witnessed something. A noise. A car. A suspicious person. And yet he hadn't seen or heard *anything*. His cabin was only four hundred feet, give or take, from the bridge. But he'd managed to sleep that night. Had the murderer known Nick was there? Was it a challenge of some kind? Nick doubted it, but he couldn't shake the feeling that it was on him to hunt down the fucker who'd decided acting like a god was his kind of fun.

In his mind, he separated the men-in-black SUV from Lizzy's killer. He'd seen the SUV—although there could have been more than one driving around—before and after Lizzy. Either the occupants were stupid and trying to be seen, or they had nothing to hide and Nick was a paranoid freak. Therefore, they had nothing to do with Lizzy Harlow.

The SUV situation bothered Nick a lot, but he didn't know what to do about it. If he reported it to the cops, they would laugh him out of the building. The Strip was a public roadway, and people could drive on it as often as they liked, day or night. And the only thing he could do for Lizzy Harlow now was to be vigilant.

"If no one else is going to pay attention," he whispered into the shadows, "it's going to have to be me."

Next time the SUV came flying through town, he'd try to find out where they went.

He finally drifted off, Kitten still on his chest. Tomorrow, he'd make her sleep in the carrier.

As luck would have it, or something less like luck and a tad closer to malevolence, Nick saw the black SUV again the next day. He was on his way to Liam's, needing time to calm down after the stupid run-in with Martin Purdy. He'd left a pissed-off Kitten safely contained in the bathroom.

The Penis Incident was brought on by his own actions, but Nick flat-out refused to explain to Purdy that his chainsaw art was so terrible it only looked phallic and wasn't actually a representation of a penis. Penis carvings could be a big seller in the right market, after all.

After slamming the door in Purdy's stupidly sexy face, he'd needed to get out of the cabin, off the property and away from the almost irresistible temptation to carve everything in sight into huge, unmistakable penises.

The storm Nick had seen lingering off the coast had finally rolled in. The wind and driving rain grew stronger and harder as he trudged along toward Liam's. Nick's gloveless hands were shoved into his coat pockets, and he hunched his shoulders, trying to make himself a smaller target for the sheeting rain. He'd just crossed The Strip when the fucking black SUV sped past, drenching him completely from head to toe.

"Motherfuckers," Nick growled, spinning and glaring after the car. Now he was going to have to ask Liam if he could use his dryer as well as hang out on his couch. Nick *hated* asking for favors, even from Liam. Asking Xavier for a ride to the veterinarian had been some kind of weird anomaly.

Squinting after it, he tried to catch the plate number, but they were already too far away for him to read it. Then brake lights flashed, and the SUV slowed and took a right turn into the neighborhood behind Pizza Mart. Cursing vehemently, Nick jogged after it, ignoring the twinge of pain in his thigh, and headed the opposite direction from Liam's house—and the clothes dryer—hoping he'd see where the SUV was headed.

By the time he got to the corner, the car wasn't in sight. Pausing and staring down the street, Nick decided to head that direction anyway. See if he could find out what was down there that creepy out-of-towners might be interested in.

Did he feel like some idiot Hardy Boys impersonator? Yes, he did.

Did he do it anyway? Yes, he did.

Cooper Springs was a long, narrow town, forced to be so by the immoveable ocean on the one side and the forest on the other. This meant Nick didn't have many blocks to go before he came to the end of the road. There was no outlet, so the SUV must have turned again down one of the earlier blocks. It was nowhere in sight.

"Fucking damn."

The only thing of interest on this street was the old Cooper Mansion, given to the city by Forrest's grandparents in the 1980s. These days, the mansion sat empty as it waited for town leaders to come up with the funds to do something with it.

There was no sign of the SUV.

This four-block neighborhood was made up of mostly older homes. Some of them had been built at the same time as the mansion, while an unfortunate cluster had been built in the nineties and were ugly as sin. A crime that had never been punished. From the outside, most of the houses in the small neighborhood seemed to be in good shape, and none had a For Sale sign in front of them. A well-worn trail off the dead-end street looked like it probably led to the high school. When Nick had gone there, he'd used a similar path on a daily basis. It was faster to cut through the edge of the woods than go all the way around.

"Huh." There was absolutely nothing suspicious that he could see.

Not wanting residents to report *him* to CSPD as a creeper, Nick turned around and headed back toward Liam's. The rain continued to fall and by the time he arrived, there wasn't a part of him that wasn't cold and wet.

NICK

Fact: Diamonds come in almost every color, but red is the rarest. There are about 30 known red diamonds in the world.

"What the hell?" Liam exclaimed after opening his front door and finding Nick doing his best impression of a drowned rat. "What happened to you?"

"It's raining, in case you hadn't noticed."

"You look like you went for a swim."

"It felt like it. Can I"—Nick looked down at himself—"uh, use your dryer? And you're gonna have to move your ass so I can get past you."

"Sure, of course." Stepping back and letting him inside, Liam peered over Nick's shoulder. "Not sure it's going to stop pissing down anytime soon though."

"A guy can hope."

Nick's clothes were heading into the spin cycle and Liam had loaned him a pair of sweats and a t-shirt for the duration. He plopped onto Liam's couch, not really sure what to do with himself, his body and brain still twitchy from the residual adrenaline running through his veins.

"You need some help?" he called out to Liam.

"Nope. I'll be right there."

Liam emerged from his kitchen carrying two steaming mugs of what Nick hoped was hot chocolate.

"Hot chocolate," Liam confirmed, handing a mug to Nick.

"Thanks. Didn't think I was going to be taking an outdoor shower today." He wrapped his fingers around the mug, soaking up its warmth.

Liam sat down next to him, making the cushions sink further. "What were you doing outside anyway?"

Nick had learned early on that he might as well be honest with Liam. Not that he was a habitual liar, but the few times he'd bent the truth, or left information out of something, Liam somehow knew about it anyway. That went all the way back to the first time they met, when Liam had come upon nine-year-old Nick crying on his front porch because he'd forgotten his house key and his parents had decided to *teach him a lesson* about responsibility.

"I got into it with Purdy, had to get some fresh air." He decided not to add that he'd also chased after a random SUV.

Liam sipped his cocoa. "Not sure you can get air any fresher right now."

Nick waited. There was no way Liam wouldn't want to know what had set him off.

"What happened?" he asked Nick, a little smile playing across his lips as if he already knew it would be something ridiculous.

"He saw my most recent carving effort and threatened to set it on fire."

"What?" Liam's blond eyebrows tried to disappear underneath his unruly hair.

Nick chuckled with pleasure. "Purdy thinks it's a penis. And no, I didn't correct him. In fact, I think I'm going to make more of them."

He was going to carve *so many dicks.*

Liam laughed. "A penis? How did that happen?"

Of course, Liam would ask that. His carvings were real art and looked like what they were supposed to look like.

"It is supposed to be a toadstool. The start of a toadstool," he amended.

"But it looks like a dick?" Setting his mug of cocoa on the coffee table, Liam let loose with a deep chuckle while he waited for Nick's response.

"I suppose so," Nick conceded, wrinkling his nose. "If you squint at it. Anyway, he said if I didn't take it down, he was gonna throw it in the fire pit and have a bonfire."

Liam wasn't just chuckling now, he was guffawing. Tears streamed from the corner of his eyes and down his cheeks.

"I mean, I was thinking about burning it too," Nick admitted, "but now I'm going to make hundreds of them. There's going to be a fairy circle of toadstool penises infesting the front lawn."

Just thinking about carving dicks galore made Nick as happy as he had been in months, maybe since before the shooting. As soon as the weather cooperated, dicks would be spouting up all over the place. He laughed along with Liam as he envisioned a forest of cock in front of the cabins.

"Are you sure," Liam asked him between gasps for air, "that you want to antagonize him?"

"Never been surer of anything in my life," Nick confirmed. For reasons he didn't feel like examining, he did not tell Liam about the kitten.

They sat quietly for a while, sipping at their hot chocolates and occasionally snickering. Nick didn't know what was going on in Liam's brain, but Nick was imagining the Cooper Springs

Resort front lawn covered with dicks big and small—some cut, some uncut—he liked all cock, after all. He chuckled again.

"The dicks, or rather, dick"—Liam laughed—"explains why you're here but not why you arrived soaked to the skin. Your place is only a mile from here. You should be drenched on just one side."

Dammit.

Nick sighed and stared up at the popcorn ceiling. *Probably some asbestos there.* The problem with Liam was that he presented as kind of a hippie space cadet, but he was the exact opposite. He *was* a hippie, if there was such a thing in the twenty-first century, but he was far from stupid. Liam was one of the most observant people Nick had ever known. Not much got past him.

"Remember a while back? When I told you guys about a car I didn't like?" Nick asked.

Liam nodded. He had an excellent memory.

"I've seen it a couple more times and today, on my way over, I saw it again. I thought I'd try and see where it was headed."

"Nick..." Liam shook his head.

"I know." He raised a hand. "You think I'm obsessing or something. Let's skip past that part, can we? It turned down the street the mansion's on. I didn't get there in time to see where it went after that, so it doesn't really matter, but that's how I got wet. That, and the jackass driver hit a puddle and doused me."

"Have you reported the truck to the police?" Liam asked.

"What are they going to do? They have enough on their hands—oh, shit." Twisting around, he stared at his friend. "Did you hear that Blair Cruz is missing?"

Liam's mouth dropped open. "What?"

"Yeah, I heard last night. The new police chief stopped by to ask if we'd seen anything, or anyone."

"How?"

Nick shrugged. "I don't really know much. Chief Dear said

that she left a weekend sleepover early, I guess. I can see her wanting to do those. If I was"—he waved a hand—"however old she is, I wouldn't want to be stuck as far out as they live."

"Well, shit." Liam huffed out a sigh. His shoulders slumped; all signs of amusement disappeared. "This is not good."

Everybody in Cooper Springs knew the tragic Cruz family story. After Levi's fisherman dad drowned, along with several others, Levi had been made guardian of his infant sister. Cooper Springs had rallied around them both with bake sales and rummage sales to help pay for Blair's upbringing. Twenty-five years old at the time, Levi had inherited his dad's property, an old farm with an adjoining apple orchard. Nick remembered his parents taking him there once, when he was a kid, for a fall festival, complete with lots of apple-related activities. He'd gotten carsick on the way home, which had not impressed his mother or father. Up until that moment, it'd been one of the better times of his childhood.

Nick couldn't fathom what Levi must be going through now. His only relative missing? Christ. Nick's family was Liam. If something happened to him, Nick would be rudderless, distraught. He wasn't comfortable even thinking that anything bad might happen to Liam.

Liam spoke, dragging Nick out of his thoughts. "Do you think it's possible this black car you keep seeing has something to do with Blair's disappearance?"

"I mean, maybe? But there's nothing solid. Probably just Crazy Nick overreacting, as usual. More likely, Blair ran away for some reason we don't know and is in Aberdeen. Or she took the bus to Seattle."

"You're not crazy, Nick. I hate it when you say that. Let's stick with peculiar."

"Peculiar Nick doesn't have the same panache."

"I dunno, I think it does." Liam smiled and waggled his eyebrows.

They went quiet again. Nick finished the last of his hot chocolate just as the dryer buzzed, so he started to ease himself up off Liam's couch.

"I think you should go to the police."

"Fuck." He fell back onto the cushions. "Liam, *no one* will believe me."

"At least tell Lani," Liam insisted.

Lani was Forrest Cooper's younger sister as well as one of Cooper Springs' finest.

Nick shivered. "She scares me."

"That's kind of her job," Liam pointed out.

"I thought it was to protect and serve," Nick mumbled.

"And scare, if needed. Lani will listen to you. She's a good cop."

Growing up as Forrest Cooper's younger sister probably helped too. She'd witnessed his shenanigans from the inside, so to speak.

"I'll think about it."

He'd think about it and then not do it. Then Liam side-swiped him with another fucking question.

"Have you decided what you want to do about the International Press? Have you looked at their offer?"

Fucking hell. Liam was not his friend. *Liam was worse than his mother*. Nick immediately took that thought back. Liam meant well. And fine, he probably knew best. But, fuck, Nick didn't know if he wanted to go back to freelancing for the IP. He'd opened his laptop just once since his return, seen the email, then immediately shut the lid again. And then made the mistake of mentioning it to his best friend.

"Ignore me," Liam said, heaving himself up off the couch. "You know what you want to do. But I think you need to stop obsessing about the car you've seen and go talk to the cops about it."

The problem was, Nick didn't have any idea what he wanted

to do—beyond the immediate ideas of creating a forest of penises and randomly hanging out with a kitten.

He was stuck in a sort of stasis he couldn't get himself out of. He kept telling himself it was because he needed more time, but he wasn't sure that was true any longer.

And he'd never admit it—*not even to Liam*—but for the past two months, ever since he'd seen Professor Martin Purdy climbing out of his car, Nick understood what it must feel like to be struck by lightning.

Repeatedly struck by lightning.

From where Nick had been lurking that first day—because *yes,* he had heard Xavier's voice message, he just hadn't given a damn—he'd watched the awestruck expression spread across Purdy's face. He'd literally seen the man fall in love with the property. Without having Xavier notify him, Nick had known at that exact moment who the new owner of the resort was going to be.

If Nick was doing any obsessing these days, it was about Professor Martin Purdy. His silver hair, the should-be-illegal t-shirts he wore, those arms that looked like they'd keep all the monsters away. The creepy SUV was fact. The SUV was *not* a figment of his imagination. Seeing Martin Purdy again after twelve years, and now wanting the man to look at Nick the same way he'd looked at the cabins, was a fantasy.

As well as a virtual punch in the stomach that left Nick breathless and pissed off.

"Hey, you coming to the thing tomorrow?" Liam asked.

Nick groaned. He'd put Magnus's annual community celebration out of his mind.

"Not if I don't have to."

NICK - FEAST DAY

Fact: Volcanic lightning occurs mostly within the cloud of ash during an eruption. It's created by the friction of the ash rushing to the earth's surface. About 200 accounts of this lightning have been witnessed live. One of these times was when Mount St. Helens erupted in 1980.

Disconnecting the power and setting his chainsaw down, Nick eyed the mushroom he'd been working on. He supposed it also looked a little like a penis, but theoretically, it was a morel. But if he squinted hard at it, the mis-formed carving could possibly be a dick. Martin Purdy had no idea what he'd unleashed.

Nick's mission to create a forest of penis-mushrooms had officially begun.

He only had enough time to carve one penis so far. One was going to have to be enough for today. If he didn't make an appearance at the pub soon, Magnus would send Rufus over to fetch him. Most people in town steered clear of him—which Nick appreciated—but Magnus, as well as Liam, *pushed*, and Nick wasn't sure what to do about that.

After cleaning up his tools and tucking them away in the

lean-to he'd built just for that purpose, Nick ducked inside his cabin.

Not *his* cabin. Merely the cabin he was lucky enough to call home for a short period of time. He didn't know what he was going to do at the end of next summer, but there was no point in thinking about that now.

Kitten meowed at him, bored from being forced to stay inside and out of the way of the chainsaw. Or maybe she had opinions about mushroom carvings that she needed to air.

"You'll live. I'll leave some food out. I won't be gone that long." A man could hope anyway.

Stripping down and leaving his clothes in a messy pile on the floor, Nick stepped into the postage-stamp-sized bathroom with its one-person shower. The water took a long time to warm up—the hot water heater was probably about to go—but Nick had endured colder showers in worse places.

He soaped himself up, doing his best to ignore the jagged scar on his thigh. It was both sensitive and numb. The last doctor he'd seen had told him he might never get all the feeling back, that there was just no way to know.

He'd barely gotten dry again when he heard someone pounding on the front door.

"I fucking hear you," he yelled, quickly pulling on a fresh pair of briefs. "Just a fucking second."

Without bothering to put on more clothes—whoever it was could just deal, and it was probably Liam anyway and he'd seen all it before—Nick crossed to the door and jerked it open. Kitten was nowhere in sight. Probably hiding under the futon; Nick kind of wished he could join her.

Martin Purdy blinked and stared at him for a second. "I'm supposed to bring you to the dinner thing at the pub," he finally said. "Magnus sent me."

Nick stared back, enjoying the prof's discomfort.

"I'll be there in a second."

Martin shook his head. "Nope. Not acceptable. I'm under strict instructions to escort you. And if I don't bring you with me, he's sending his dad."

A gust of wind blew in the door. Nick shivered. Martin's eyes narrowed.

"Quit being a stubborn ass and get dressed. The sooner we get over there, the sooner you can ignore me."

"Fine," Nick growled and slammed the door shut.

He'd hoped Martin would take a hint and leave for the pub by the time he was dressed. No such luck. When Nick opened the door again, Martin was still there, leaning against the siding with his hands tucked into his parka's pockets. Looking fucking sexy. Which was all sorts of wrong.

Pulling the door closed behind him and jiggling the handle to make sure it was locked, Nick started toward the path down the hill to The Strip. Magnus could send Martin to get Nick, but it didn't mean he had to talk to him.

Another memo that Purdy didn't pay any attention to.

"What have you got against me, anyway?" Martin asked. "We don't know each other. I just moved from Seattle, and from what I've heard, you were traveling the world while I tried to teach uninterested students about rocks."

Nick clenched his jaw. He was not going to confess to Martin Purdy that he'd failed his class and thus failed out of college, that he'd been living with the consequences of all of it for over a decade. He sucked in a breath to dampen the anger, mostly shame, that he still felt at the memory.

"Not going to tell me, huh? It shouldn't bother me that you have this grudge, but it does. I'm not used to people just... hating me." Martin sounded confused, like maybe no one had ever hated him before.

They'd reached the two-lane road that cut through Cooper Springs, and Nick waited for a truck to pass before he crossed and started walking faster.

"You do know we're going to the same place, right?" Martin asked, not sounding a bit out of breath.

Nick didn't reply. Martin didn't let him draw ahead, he just stayed even with Nick and even pushed ahead at the very end and pulled the door open before Nick could do it himself.

The Donkey was comfortably crowded. Nick could name everyone inside, which was a plus, and most of them left him alone, which was even better. Magnus and his staff had moved all the free-standing tables to the middle of the room, making one long row. Then they'd covered them with white tablecloths to create a long banquet. People could sit at the tables or break off and sit in the booths.

The booths and the tables lined up in the center all had vases filled with dried flower arrangements on them, and overhead played Magnus's favorite instrumental Celtic soundtrack. All in all, it was a nice setup. If Nick hadn't been so irritated, he might have appreciated it more.

Ditching Martin, Nick headed to the corner booth where Liam was sitting across from Silas Murphy, owner-operator of the auto shop. Nick didn't know Silas well, only that he was quiet to a fault. Hardly ever spoke unless he was spoken to first. Liam claimed it was because he spent entire days with his head under the hoods of all the cars and trucks in the area. Frankly, Nick appreciated someone who didn't run their mouth constantly.

"Liam, Silas." Peeling off his coat, Nick moved to sit next to Liam. "Scoot over, asshole."

Liam's dimple popped as he repressed a grin. But he moved over and Nick shoved in next to him.

"That was good of you to walk over with Purdy," Liam commented.

For about half a second, Nick felt guilty about Purdy, but he pushed it aside. He didn't owe him anything, especially not his friendship. Liam, ever the mind reader, must have seen something in his expression.

"You *didn't* walk over with him, did you? Jeez, Nick, lighten up already. What did the guy ever do to you? Are you still mad about the penis thing?"

Nick's gaze flicked across the table to Silas, who looked amused and curious. He dipped his head as if to say, "Go ahead."

"*No.* I mean, yes, I am pissed about the mushrooms. But he's *the one*," Nick growled. He hadn't told anyone the name of the professor who'd sent him the email all those years ago about failing his class. He'd felt so incredibly stupid. After being told he was stupid and a failure all his life, he had actually *failed.*

Having Purdy show up in his life again, after what felt to him like a second failure—not the getting shot, but what happened afterward, the crawling back to Cooper Springs with nothing to show for himself—was rubbing salt in the wound.

Nick was tired to the bone.

The therapist he'd seen for all of four sessions claimed Nick used anger to protect himself, then had suggested he try thinking about times he'd been happy and holding onto that feeling, even if it was just for a few minutes.

She hadn't been impressed with his answer, and he hadn't gone back. But maybe she had a point. Why was it easier to hold on to anger than happiness? Was he somehow broken?

As always, Liam dragged him out of his morose thoughts. "The one what? Or who, rather?" he asked.

"He's the one whose class I was failing before—*you know.*"

Before Nick had fled the country to avoid the wrath of his parents and the mockery of people he'd thought were his friends. Except for Liam, who truly was a friend.

"Oooh." Dawning understanding had Liam nodding his head.

They all stared across the room. Martin had taken his coat

off and draped it over one arm. He was talking to Rufus, who laughed and took his coat, hanging it along with several others on a wall hook near the end of the bar.

"Did you ever talk to him back in the day?" Liam asked.

Nick shook his head. "Why? There was no point. I was done."

"Mm-hmm. Nick, I've known you a long time. Almost all my life." The gleam in Liam's agate green eyes made Nick wary. Liam may not have gone to Harvard, but he was damn smart. "I've known you to overreact, jump to conclusions." He raised a hand to keep Nick from arguing. "I just think it would be odd for a teacher to just email you that you were going to fail his class, so, hey, give up."

It had been over twelve years, but Nick had The Email memorized. Nightmares—the only dreams he had—always had a slow scene where he was innocently checking his school inbox only to see the doom-laden word *failing*. Some people dreamed about forgetting their locker combination; Nick had nightmares about an email.

"Maybe he'd been trying to help," Liam suggested. "Maybe he'd sent the email so you could find tutoring or something?"

"I seriously doubt it," Nick scoffed, even as he wondered to himself if that had been the case. "Besides, my parents wouldn't have cared and wouldn't have paid for tutoring anyway, you know that." His parents had made it clear from the very beginning that failure was not an option.

Michael and Jerri Waugh did not suffer fools and had spent Nick's childhood bemoaning the fact that they'd had a fool for a son. Their only son. Their only child. Who should have been perfect because he was their spawn. Instead, he was horribly imperfect and a constant source of embarrassment.

After Nick graduated from high school, they'd moved across the country to Florida where Nick's aunt and uncle lived, as if knowing he was going to fail college and needing to distance themselves from his humiliation. Or, alternatively, as if they couldn't wait to separate their existence from his.

Magnus approached the booth, carrying three pints of beer. Without disrupting the conversation, he set one down in front of each of them and departed.

"Thanks for the beer," Nick said.

"Magnus is buying tonight," Silas said quietly. "He better not expect me to fix all the cars in town for free."

Nick eyed Silas. Was that a joke? It was hard to tell with him.

"I've always wondered why your parents ever had a kid," Liam began, obviously not ready to just drop the damn subject.

"Hell if I know," Nick grumbled. "They must've thought it was their duty, something you did when you got married."

"Remember that one time when I stayed over?" Liam glanced across the table at Silas. "Seriously, the only time I ever stayed over. We were downstairs messing around. All of a sudden, this disembodied voice comes out of nowhere. *'Nicholas, it's time to come upstairs to tell your father goodnight.'* Nick's folks had intercoms installed so they wouldn't have to make the trip downstairs or anywhere. If they wanted him, they summoned him through this thing. I dunno, it really bugged me."

Nick nodded; he'd hated being summoned by the intercoms.

"So, I don't know if I ever told you, Nick. I followed after you but stopped at the top of the stairs. Honestly, I don't think I've been as weirded-out before or since." Liam glanced over at Silas. "Nick's dad had this whacked-out throne-like chair. He waved for Nick to come close like he was king and Nick was a… a mere supplicant. Nick had to stand in front of him and say goodnight, then kiss him on the cheek. His dad asked a few questions, then Nick kissed his mother on the cheek. I snuck back downstairs, and you showed up a few minutes later."

Huh. Liam had never told him this. It explained why they always hung out at Liam's house after that.

"They didn't kiss him back or even hug him," Liam continued. "Fucking creepy as hell."

Nick agreed with Liam, but he hadn't known any better at the time. Now he knew that most parents did not summon their children like they were servants.

"I didn't know you saw that. But yeah, that's just one reason why staying at your place was so much better."

Liam, on the other hand, grew up in what Liam's moms jokingly called "the lesbian commune"—a family farm outside of town where several lesbian couples lived. They raised goats and pigs, grew veggies for the household, and made craft soaps and other stuff they sold at markets and online. They'd even had a horse that Nick had ridden a few times.

"Dad always asked the same questions," Nick added. "How school was, whether I finished my homework, and what the grade on my last test was."

Liam threw up his hands and flopped backward, shaking the booth. "See?"

Silas nodded as he picked at the coaster in front of him. "No offense, seems kind of odd to me." The comment was followed by Silas's cheeks turning bright red, as if he thought he'd gone too far.

"None taken," Nick assured Silas while he wondered at Silas's reaction. "None at all. It was totally fucked up."

"Anyway, Nick," Liam said, "back to what I was getting to before we went on the parental detour. Which is, maybe give Purdy a chance?"

Give Martin Purdy a chance? Nick gave Liam his best scowl. Why the hell would Nick want to do that? In Nick's experience, giving people a chance meant they fucked with him. Not that Purdy had done any such thing—yet. The reality was Purdy could have fought the lease the Davies children had given Nick and probably won, seeing as it had been a verbal agreement and not a signed document, but he hadn't.

"He doesn't even remember me."

That comment earned Nick a pointy elbow jammed into his ribs. "Ow. What the fuck was that for?" He rubbed his side dramatically.

"Of course he doesn't remember you, moron. How many students do you think he's had over the years? I remember you telling me how huge your classes were. Dude," Liam finished with a disappointed headshake.

Nick opened his mouth to protest further, but he was stalled by Magnus, who was now standing at the head of the banquet.

"Evening, everyone. I won't keep you..." Magnus paused because there was a rumble of *quit talking, let us eat then, hurry up, old man*, and other comments. Magnus was used to the friendly abuse. "The more crap you all give me, the longer I'm gonna talk," he warned them with an evil grin. The crowd quieted again. "That's more like it. Thank you all for coming, even if I had to twist a few arms." He glanced over at the booth Nick, Silas, and Liam occupied. "We are nothing without our community. Thank you to the old-timers for continuing to stay in town and supporting small businesses here, to the younger generation who hasn't quite given up yet, and lastly, welcome to the newcomers—the newest newcomer. Before we eat, let's raise our glasses to our future."

"Let's hope the future doesn't get drunk and fuck everything up," someone murmured into the silence. The comment was met with laughter and agreement as everyone began eating.

Not long later, Nick leaned back against the back of the booth with a massive sigh. He was both full and satisfied. He'd have been more satisfied if Magnus hadn't instilled a ridiculous round-robin rule and forced everyone to move to a new seat and chat with someone else every half hour.

Being contrary, Nick had refused to move, but Liam and Silas had abandoned him. He'd then been joined by Critter and Mags, the two Forest Service officers. Everyone in town suspected they were a couple, but Nick figured it was none of his business what the two got up to in their spare and private time.

"You ready for the storm?" Critter asked him, rolling a toothpick around his mouth.

Critter was about Nick's height and had the leanness of someone who'd never had a desk job. Mags was short and curvy, but Nick knew from experience that she could hike for miles and not break a sweat. She normally kept her curly black hair in braids but tonight she'd let them free—her words—and Nick found himself staring at the cloud of dark hair that moved when Mags talked.

"Ah. What storm?" Nick was the only adult he knew who didn't own a cell phone; the cabin had a working landline, so he didn't see a need. It wasn't like he wanted to talk to people, and he could always just look outside to see the weather. His powered-off laptop stayed shut down in the cabin, where he'd been successfully avoiding it for months.

"Oh," Mags added, waving her hand, "you know, the usual post-holiday storm. Forecasters are saying this one will hit the coast tomorrow afternoon, and they're predicting higher than normal winds," she informed him with glee. "And," she whispered, "there's a king tide, the highest of the year. Critter and I are gonna hunker down in one of the observatories."

"Huh. I had no idea."

He wondered if Purdy knew about the upcoming weather and decided it didn't matter if he did or not. The weather was still going to happen. His attention drifted to the bar, where Martin sat chatting with Wanda Stone and Rufus.

Not that Nick was keeping an eye on him or anything.

The fact that he knew Martin had been through the buffet line twice and had already drunk a stout and some sort of pale ale was pure chance. It looked like he was having a good time.

Nick was enjoying this chance to watch him without Martin being aware of it.

It irritated him that he had a difficult time focusing on anything else when Martin Purdy was in the room. Just like twelve years ago, when he couldn't remember the difference between an igneous rock and a metamorphic rock because the hot older guy teaching the class was distractingly good-looking.

"How is the new guy?" Critter asked, interrupting Nick's perusal of Martin's thick biceps and muscly chest.

For a moment, Nick wondered what Critter was talking about. Then he cocked his head toward the bar.

Oh, right.

Nick dragged his attention back to his table partners. "Uh. He's only been here for what, four days? It's early yet." Crap, had Critter busted him staring? Surely, they were about to move along to a new table? He mentally crossed his fingers.

"You haven't talked to him?" Mags asked.

Nick shrugged. Mags had this way of meaning more than she actually said. No, he hadn't greeted Martin Purdy with a house-warming gift or even helped him and his friends unload the moving truck.

"Not really."

"Critter," Mags said as she turned to her partner, "we need to do something for him. The poor man is going to think Cooper Springs is the worst town ever." She paused thoughtfully. "Maybe after the storm passes, I'll put together a seafood pie and one of us will drop it over."

Full or not, Nick's mouth started to water at the mention of Mags's seafood pie. But almost as if Mother Nature had been eavesdropping on their conversation, the pendant lights overhead flickered and went out. A second later, they came back on. The din of conversation rose as just about everyone stood up and started to help Magnus and Garth clear tables and return dishes to the kitchen.

Thirty minutes later, Magnus and Rufus were shooing them out the door and telling everyone they'd take care of the rest and to please stay safe.

"If it gets bad overnight or tomorrow and you need shelter, we'll be here. This building has withstood a lot more than a pokey winter storm." Magnus said something else as he stood at the pub's door, but his words were snatched away by the wind.

Outside, Nick couldn't believe the difference in the weather in only a few hours. He had grown up in Cooper Springs and experienced the late fall weather shifts before, but it still surprised him, even if living so close to the ocean meant there was always wind at this time of year.

It was gusting now, maybe twenty miles an hour or more, causing the power lines to swing back and forth. One hundred yards to the south, the town's single stoplight bounced and swayed like a yo-yo. The red light reflected in the watery pavement, changing to green and then yellow again as Nick stood still, entranced by the gale.

"I had no idea a storm was heading our way." Purdy's deep voice at his ear shocked Nick. "Makes me extra glad I had that generator installed. But also feeling like an idiot for not paying attention to the forecast." He flicked up his hood and tugged the zipper on his jacket up to his neck. "And it makes me wish I'd driven. We're going to be soaking by the time we get back." He glanced at Nick. "We might as well get going."

He stepped away from the semi-protection the brick wall of the Steam Donkey provided. The wind immediately began pushing against his strong form, tugging at Martin's parka and defining his broad shoulders and biceps. Nick grunted, irritated that Martin just expected him to follow.

Where else would you go?

On the other hand, Purdy's solid body would provide a bit of a windbreak.

Gritting his teeth, Nick followed Martin Purdy into the

storm, jogging to catch up with him. They finally arrived at Martin's cabin ten minutes later. Nick was freezing and soaked, regardless of his rain gear, and Martin probably was too, but Nick didn't ask him. He kept moving, eager to get inside his own cabin and away from the frustrating temptation of Martin Purdy.

"Nick!"

Nick slowed but didn't turn back around.

"If you need anything, you know where I am," Martin called to his back.

MARTIN - FRIDAY

Fact: Rocks aren't always solid. Sand and mud are also rocks. No matter where you are, you can't escape rocks.

Martin sat back on the couch with a glass of whiskey in his hand, listening as the wind howled and lamented outside. A flash of lightning illuminated the living room for half a second, then thunder boomed and crashed less than a second later, sounding like it was directly over the cabin. Goose bumps formed on his arms and Martin realized he was smiling. He *loved* storms.

It would have been nice if this one hadn't taken him by surprise; he felt unprepared. After jogging back from the pub—not so much *with* as *at the same time as* Nick—he'd done what he could to plan for the storm he hadn't known was coming.

"What an idiot," he grumbled.

He wasn't in the city anymore, with convenience stores and everything they had to offer, so he needed to be mindful of the elements. It was reckless and he'd been caught unawares. And he was damn lucky the electrician had been able to hook up the generator.

Water was the only thing he was truly concerned about. After getting home, he'd dug out several coolers and the container he used when he went camping, then filled them up. The house didn't have a bathtub, so the coolers would have to do. Might be a good idea to see if he could source a tub that would fit in the small bathroom, one that he would fit in as well.

The gale buffeted the cabin, testing the windows and trying to creep inside through gaps in the siding. Drinking the last of his whiskey, Martin forced himself up off the couch and headed into his bedroom to change into sleep pants, a thick sweatshirt, and wool socks. If worse came to worst and the roof blew off, he didn't want to be mostly naked.

Fingers crossed, it didn't come to that. Simon and Charley would never let him forget it. He plucked his phone off the bedside table. As he suspected, there was no service. He still had internet though. Thank god; the generator was paying off in more ways than one.

Big storm tonight but all's well, he typed. Then he felt like a teenager checking in with his parents and erased it. He'd call them in the morning.

He'd also been tempted to check on Waugh and reiterate his offer of help if he needed anything, but Martin predicted he would not be receptive. He just had to trust that, if something did happen in the night, Nick would come to him.

For reasons he hadn't tried to understand, Martin felt protective of the younger man, an inexplicable instinct to keep him safe.

From what, Martin?

That was an unanswerable question. Maybe just the world in

general. He reminded Martin of a feral animal, a cat or dog who'd never received or expected kindness.

He shook his head. Definitely a cat.

Even if it was in Nick's best interest to accept help, Martin suspected he would rather tough it out. Hopefully, he wouldn't need assistance anytime soon because Martin didn't trust Nick to ask for it.

There was nothing Martin could do about that—other than answer the door if Nick knocked.

Throwing back the covers, Martin crawled into bed and lay on his back, staring at the ceiling. He was full from all the food he'd stuffed himself with at the Donkey. And all the conversation too. Martin hadn't expected to be the center of attention, but townspeople he hadn't met practically lined up at his table to greet him. There were worse ways to meet folks. He supposed that he'd gotten a lot of the handshaking over with.

Chief Dear hadn't been there, or any of the rest of the CSPD, but maybe he wouldn't recognize them in street clothes. He hoped that meant progress was being made on the missing girl.

Everyone he'd talked to had been welcoming as well as kind, even if he felt like a bit of an imposter. He'd moved to Cooper Springs for purely selfish reasons, and many of the town residents he'd met seemed to expect him to pull off some kind of miracle and revive the long-dead tourist trade.

If the tourist trade increased, great. But Martin wasn't betting his farm on it. He'd left Seattle and come to Cooper Springs because it *felt right* to him. And between his own savings, the sale of his house, and the money his aunt had left him, he fully owned the "resort." Or maybe it owned him, knowing the repairs he had to look forward to.

Rain continued to pummel against the roof, distracting him from hazy thoughts of the future. What he needed right now was for the roof over his head to hold until the roofers came out to replace it and the rest of the cabins' roofs. With these thoughts swirling in his head, Martin drifted off into a light sleep.

Wind and rain pounded against the house, from every side all at once, demanding to be let in. He begged the wind to be quiet, but it ignored him.

Fuck.

Martin came awake with a start and sat bolt upright. The pounding he heard came from the front of the house. Throwing back the covers and leaping out of bed, he rushed out to the living room—incredibly, he managed not to trip on any boxes he'd left out—and threw open the door.

A shivering and shirtless Nick Waugh stood on the other side. Rainwater dripped down his face, his hair was plastered to his head, and his hands were clutching a t-shirt to his chest. He looked a great deal like a half-drowned cat.

"Get in here," Martin commanded, hurrying him inside and shutting the door behind him. "What the hell happened?" he demanded. "Here," he said before Nick could answer him, "wrap up in this." He tossed Nick a throw blanket he'd left draped over the back of the couch.

Nick didn't catch the coverlet, so it slipped to the floor as the rainwater continued to drip down his bare chest. Martin shot him an exasperated stare. Snatching up the blanket, he wrapped it around Nick's shoulders. Martin could feel the cold coming off his skin.

"What happened? Are you hurt?"

Nick shook his head, finally responding. "I didn't kn-kn-ow where else to go." His body shook again as he tried to warm up. "T-t-tree." His teeth clattered together, and Nick's lips were blue with cold. "F-fell. M-mostly m-m-missed the c-c-cabin, b-but some b-b-big b-b-branches didn't." He took a deep breath that seemed to settle his words a bit. "The roof is caved in. I, I, uh, I'm not sure how much damage there really is."

Jesus fucking Christ, hadn't Martin *just hours ago* told Nick to come to him if he needed anything? Was he incapable of accepting basic human kindness?

"I don't fucking care about damage to the cabins. They can be repaired. *Are you hurt?*" He barely managed to restrain himself from grabbing Nick and running his hands down his person to search for injury. It surprised him that he wished he could do just that. Martin forced his brain to swerve away from what would be a Bad Move.

Nick shook his head again. If Martin didn't know better, he might have thought Nick had taken a midnight swim in the ocean with just his pajama bottoms on. The useless rag was still pressed against his chest as he shivered violently.

Martin held his hand out. "Let me have that so you can hold the blanket better. We need to warm you up."

Nick stared at him, his eyes wide, but let Martin peel the wet fabric from his grip.

It squeaked and a tiny orange ball with ears poked its head out.

"A kitten?" Martin's voice softened. "Oh, it's cold too. We need to warm both of you up." The kitten tried to bite him. Martin laughed even though the situation was serious. "Figures your cat would try and bite me."

A clean kitchen rag lay folded on the top of a stack of towels he hadn't found a home for yet. Ignoring its violent protestations, Martin did the best he could to dry the small cat. When he was done, its orange and white fur stood straight up from its body, much like Nick's hair had the other day.

He set it down on the couch. The fuzzball meowed at him one last time before backing up into a corner and continuing to shoot him a poisonous glare. Whatever had happened, the kitten seemed fine.

"Is there anything you need tonight?" he asked Nick. "Anything we need to try and get to?" Martin didn't want to go out in the storm, but he would.

Nick shook his head.

Martin narrowed his eyes at his midnight guest. He figured Nick was in shock and had no idea if he had things that should be rescued because he was too busy failing at trying to wrap his head around nearly being mashed by a tree. The man was still ashen and his pupils were dilated. It had to be shock, seeing as he hadn't snarled or argued in the five minutes he'd been in Martin's presence. Martin preferred snarly Nick to this passive one.

"I'm going to start you a shower," he informed Nick. "Get in and take as long as you need to get warm, use all the hot water, I don't care. I'll scare up some fresh towels and find something to keep you warm tonight. The kitten will be fine for a few minutes."

His thought that Nick was not in his right mind was confirmed when Nick headed toward the bathroom without resistance. Martin beat him there and pulled back the curtain, turning the hot water on high. The small space started to fill with steam.

"There, in you go."

Martin hadn't known Nick Waugh long, but he knew him well enough to know his normal reaction was to take issue with everything and to ask questions later—possibly.

He was definitely in shock.

Nick crowded into the bathroom after Martin and dropped the banket to the linoleum flooring. Retrieving the throw, Martin exited before Nick started to remove his sopping pants. Not that he needed a good imagination to envision what was underneath the thin material, but he shouldn't ogle a likely hypothermic man.

When he heard the clink of the shower curtain being pulled

shut, Martin opened the door and set two clean towels on the toilet lid before backing out into the living room again.

"Do I want to know where you came from?" he asked the kitten. All he got in response was a twitch of one ear. Setting the throw blanket down, he pulled one edge of it over the tiny form. The heating pad he'd been teasing Simon about was also sitting out, so Martin plugged it in and eased it underneath the kitten. "There."

With the kitten ignoring him and Nick in the shower—and to distract himself from a slew of unasked-for images featuring a wet and naked Nick Waugh—Martin decided to check the damage to the other cabin. Pulling on his rain gear, Martin stepped into the tall, bright yellow rubber boots Charley had given him as a joke.

"Don't move," he said to the tiny lump on the couch. The lump continued to ignore him.

He spotted his flashlight on the mantle, grabbed it, and headed out into the storm.

The wind howled and roared, doing its best to scare the bejeezus out of anything and everyone. He hadn't bothered with a hat and good thing, too, or it would've been snatched off his head. Waves he couldn't see smashed and pounded onto the sandy beach so hard that the ground under his feet vibrated. He sensed the storm hadn't quite reached its peak yet, but it was damn close.

Sticking close to the cabins, he carefully made his way to the end of the row where Cabin Five stood.

Partially stood.

"Holy shit." Heedless of the rain, he stopped in his tracks and stared, trying to process the damage. His heart pounded frantically against his ribs as he realized just how close Nick had come to death. How had he not been injured?

The fallen tree had to have been approaching sixty feet tall. *Thank fuck*, it had missed most of the cabin, landing along the gravel drive and taking out a smaller tree with it. Nick could easily have been crushed to death while he slept. The flashlight illuminated the spot where the tree's lower boughs had caught the edge of the cabin's roof, pushing it off the walls and smashing one corner.

"Shit, fuck," Martin muttered, moving again and swinging the flashlight back and forth as he assessed the damage. The rain was coming at him sideways, and trees creaked and swayed. It was probably pretty stupid to be standing out there waiting for another damn tree to fall or for random debris to fly past him and take his head along for the ride.

He hadn't survived a heart attack just to be killed by a fucking tree.

One last time, Martin directed the flashlight beam across the remains of the cabin, hardly able to believe Nick had survived relatively unscathed—and damn glad he had. He'd sort of hoped to see if there was anything of Nick's that could be saved tonight, anything he could rescue and return to safety like some sort of slicker-clad, yellow-booted knight in shining armor. And no, he wasn't going to parse out why that role appealed. Regardless, any salvage work would have to wait until the storm passed.

Minutes later, he was back inside his own house; the shower was still running, and the feline guest still slept. Martin stripped off his sopping weather gear and hung it across one of several boxes he hadn't unpacked yet. In the kitchen, he checked the clock, which told him it was two-fifteen a.m.

There was a long way to go before daylight.

Grabbing the kettle, he held it under the faucet, and when it was full, he set it on the stove to heat. The shower water turned off while he was digging around in the cupboards, looking for the herbal tea that he knew he had somewhere.

Moving is a pain in the ass.

"Ah-hah!" Martin exclaimed when he finally spotted the orange and black box.

Seconds later, Nick padded into the kitchen. Turning around to face him, Martin took a long look at The State of Nick. The spare sweats and cotton sweater Martin had left for him were rolled up once at his wrists and ankles and—although Martin would never say anything—Nick was just enough smaller than him that, in Martin's clothing, he really did resemble an almost-drowned cat.

The shocked, almost vacant, expression from earlier had been replaced by his usual scowl. The scowl had Martin wanting to smile. He manfully resisted the temptation; Martin didn't have a death wish.

"Tea?"

Nick shrugged at the same time that the kettle whistled. The shrill sound was somewhat muffled by a gale doing its best to drown out everything but its own voice. With Nick watching, Martin poured the hot water into two mugs and dropped in the waiting tea bags. Setting the kettle back on the stove, Martin breathed in the scent of orange peel, cinnamon, and clove, then held his breath for a second before releasing it. Martin always found the Market Spice blend comforting, and he figured they both needed comfort right now.

"Are you… sniffing tea?" Nick asked, managing to sound astonished and judgmental at the same time.

Martin didn't bother to reply. He simply handed Nick one of the mugs.

"Let it steep a few minutes before you drink it."

Accepting the mug, Nick eyed it skeptically.

"Do you not like tea?" Martin asked. Personally, he only liked herbal tea; black tea hurt his stomach.

"I like tea just fine. I'm still wrapping my head around a tree trying to crawl into bed with me."

"We'll sort it out tomorrow. Or," he clarified as a particularly strong gust buffeted the cabin, "when the storm dies down."

While watching Nick wrinkle his nose but still sip the hot tea, Martin began trying to solve the problem of where Nick would sleep for the next few hours. The only comfortable solution was Martin's bed. The flooring throughout the cabin was hardwood, and the couch was a two-seater, barely sixty inches long. And while he had located his coolers, Martin still didn't know where he'd put his sleeping bag and cushy pad.

Nick wasn't as broad as Martin, being lean rather than muscled, but he was almost as tall. Trying to sleep on the couch would be torture. And trying to sleep sitting up was ridiculous when there was a perfectly good, large bed.

"Drink up and we'll try to get some rest for a few hours. I have a king bed that will fit the both of us," Martin told Nick.

"Wha—" Nick sputtered, choking on the sip of tea he'd just taken. His knuckles whitened as he gripped the mug. "No."

"Can you just not argue about this tonight?" Martin asked. "The floor is hard and cold. The couch is too short for either of us. In the morning—if we wake up in one piece—you can argue with me until you're blue in the face. But right now, I'd just like to get a couple hours of sleep. I have a feeling we're going to have a busy day."

Nick stared at him. Martin had no idea what was going on behind those stormy eyes of his. That was a lie; he had a suspicion Nick was working up some old-fashioned outrage.

"No. I'll sleep on the couch. The cat will keep me company, and I've slept in worse places."

Martin opened his mouth to try and change Nick's mind but decided against it. "You know what? I don't care where you sleep. I'm going back to bed."

He left the kitchenette, taking his tea with him. He wasn't going to force Nick Waugh to do anything. Suggesting his bed probably *was* a bit weird, but not to a guy who'd been on plenty of digs where sleeping situations had often been make-do. It wasn't as if he had a linen closet full of spare bedding. In the spring maybe, when the cabins were up and running, but not tonight. And not anytime soon.

Climbing back into his own very comfortable bed, Martin scooted to the far side just in case Nick changed his stubborn-ass mind. He chuckled; it was more likely Bigfoot would share his bed before Nick. Was the mythical beast a top, a bottom, or vers?

He sipped at his tea, enjoying the spicy flavors and the warmth of it because it had been fucking cold outside, and listened for Nick. But he heard nothing over the wind. When his tea was gone, Martin set the empty mug on the windowsill and turned onto his side, knowing he probably wouldn't fall deeply asleep but that shutting his eyes for a few hours would help.

The power finally went out a few hours later, but less than a minute after, the new generator kicked in. Martin knew this because he'd given up trying to sleep and had been dozing to the latest Jack Reacher audiobook when the bedside lamp flickered off, leaving just the red light of the fire alarm on the ceiling. He'd waited, fingers crossed, for the generator to turn on and pumped his fist when it did.

No surprise, Nick had not accepted his offering of a comfortable spot to sleep. Hopefully, he'd stayed instead of deciding that being out in the storm was better than being anywhere near Martin. What the hell was with that anyway? Flipping the duvet off his body, he got out of bed for the second time since midnight.

Martin headed to the kitchen, needing coffee. Passing the couch, he paused and eyed the somewhat-welcome sight of Nick asleep with the content kitten smack in the middle of his chest. There was no way Nick's back wasn't going to hurt when he woke up. His head was awkwardly propped up on one end and his feet hung over the other. Martin would need several sessions at the chiropractors after a night—or even an hour—in that position. And damn, without the drawn-together eyebrows and constant frown, Nick Waugh was a damn good-looking man.

This is not good.

Martin's heart rate increased as the implication of the thought washed over him. He'd been doing a good job of ignoring his low-key attraction to the prickly younger man. This turn of events was not okay. He hadn't been remotely attracted to anyone since Joe. He'd kind of figured he was done with romance.

Not that he wanted romance with his unconscious visitor.

Nick snuffled. His long, straight nose twitched, and his wide mouth looked as if it might want to smile while Nick wasn't awake enough to scowl. His dark blond eyebrows naturally flared upward at the end, much like a bird's wing.

Martin's cock twitched, and he literally stopped breathing for a second. Hell, no. He could not be attracted to this… this *feral human.*

He did his best to squash his reaction by bringing up memories of food poisoning and oh, yes, his heart attack. No matter how good-looking he was, Nick Waugh was out of bounds, a no think-feel-touch zone Martin could not violate.

Heart attack, Martin reminded himself, even as he was *still* standing there staring at Nick. Pain like nothing he'd ever felt before. The inability to draw in a breath. Being hooked up to IVs and machines that beeped and glowed as his heart righted itself again.

Martin wasn't looking for a partner. Or even a hookup. Right? *He wasn't.*

After the breakup with Joe, Martin had been too busy teaching and running the department to date. Which had been Joe's complaint in the first place, that he never came first in

Martin's world. The heart attack had changed all that—although Joe was long gone by then. Martin rubbed at his chest, worrying away the phantom pain.

Nick shifted and flung one arm over his head, moaning quietly, as if he was having a bad dream. The cat slept on. While it was tempting to shake Nick awake and ask if he was okay, Martin decided against it. But his dick still hadn't gotten the memo and stirred again. Touching Nick in any way would be a Very Bad Idea.

And a good way to earn a punch in the face.

Thankful for the generator advice Xavier had given him, as well as Electrician Rob's scheduling finesse, Martin abandoned ogling his tenant and moved into the kitchen where the espresso machine beckoned.

He made no attempt to be quiet, although he also didn't bang pots and pans like his father had when Martin had been in high school. Dad had always insisted he didn't mean to be loud, but Martin knew it was his way of getting him up for school.

His back was to the kitchen entrance and he was just steaming the milk for his coffee when Martin felt Nick's presence behind him.

"Coffee?" he asked without turning around. He'd gotten out bagels and cream cheese and had cut up a fresh tomato, arranging the selection on a plate that now sat on the table.

For a moment, there was no answer except for the wind, which thankfully was calming down. Then Martin heard Nick's gruff, "Yeah."

"Milk?"

Filling the portafilter with freshly ground beans, Martin flipped on the water switch and watched as the dark liquid began to spill into the mug he'd gotten out for Nick.

"Sure. And some for, um, the cat?"

"Help yourself to a bowl or whatever you need, and some breakfast."

"I'm okay," Nick insisted. But his stomach growled, making the words a lie.

It took everything Martin had not to growl back at him like an alpha wolf, insisting he eat.

"Have a damn bagel." There. He'd managed to be civil.

Heaven forbid, Nick accept too much from him. Heaven forbid, Martin should want Nick to accept something, anything, from him.

He added hot water to the espresso, poured the warm frothy milk into Nick's mug, and handed the concoction to him. Their fingers brushed, and Martin let his linger a beat too long. Nick's blue eyes flashed up to his, making Martin wonder if he'd felt the same shock of lust Martin had.

He suspected the answer was yes. But he couldn't go there. He wouldn't take advantage. Although the idea that Nick would let anyone take advantage of him was laughable.

Grabbing a small bowl, Martin poured the extra warm milk into it and set it on the floor. The kitten, who Nick had been holding, squeaked and demanded to be let down. They both watched as it stuck its entire face into the container.

"Thanks." The word sounded slightly less surly than Martin expected.

"How's your back?" he asked as he leaned back against the counter.

The kitchen was barely big enough for the two of them and the cat. It was more the size of a kitchenette, but Martin had never imagined he might be sharing it with another person.

Nick grimaced as he shifted his stance and stretched. "About what you'd expect."

He looked tired, and Martin wasn't surprised to note the dark circles under his eyes. Abruptly, he remembered what Forrest had said about Nick getting shot and wondered if that had been the cause of his bad dream, or if it had been something else.

The kitchen was also too small for a true kitchen table. Instead, Martin had hunted down one designed for small spaces, one that could be expanded or folded down and out of the way. With one side tucked down and the other up, the little table fit perfectly under the kitchen window. He'd also found wooden folding chairs that could be stored away when he didn't need them.

"Take a seat. Make yourself a bagel." The second part was more of an order than an invitation. "I'll grab the other chair."

Setting his coffee down on the table, Martin left the kitchen. When he returned with the chair, Nick was, amazingly, sitting down, the cat in his lap while they both stared out the window. In his hand, Nick held a bagel with a big bite out of it.

The view looked to the northwest. If it hadn't still been mostly dark out, they could've seen the line of cabins and the top of the hill that looked down over the beach. Trees still swayed with the wind but much less frenetically than last night. The storm was dying down. Thank goodness for that.

"So, where'd the kitten come from?"

"I found her on the beach the other day. Don't worry," he said quickly. "I'll find a home for her."

Martin eyed the kitten, who was ineffectively cleaning her face. "I like cats, been thinking about getting one." He'd had the thought once and hadn't followed up. This might be an easy, sensible solution.

Nick gripped the cat protectively, as if Martin was going to rip her out of his hands, and she mewed in protest. *Sure, he was going to find someone to take her.* Somehow, it didn't surprise Martin that Nick had been adopted by a tiny stubborn kitten; it was the most appropriate pairing he could imagine.

"I can't believe I didn't know there was a storm coming." Martin changed the subject, sitting down again and picking up his mug. Probably best to drop the subject of the cat.

"And a king tide," Nick added after he swallowed his bite of bagel. "Not that it will bother us up here, but there're probably some folks regretting their waterfront property."

"I hadn't thought of that. Do you think there'll be damage in town? Who should we check in with?"

Nick's eyebrows drew together in a familiar manner. "Probably, someone will check on you first. Seeing as you're the new guy."

New guy definitely had a *tone* to it.

"Huh. Well, I suppose I should finish my coffee and get ready to check the damage." He glanced out the window again to see it was just starting to lighten. "I think it's safe enough now. I doubt there will be tree limbs flying around."

Nick grunted. Martin decided to take it as agreement.

They finished their coffee and breakfast in silence. Martin wasn't going to force conversation, but at least Nick was eating something. Rising to his feet, Martin set his mug in the sink to wash later.

"I'm getting dressed." He eyed Nick. "I doubt any of my jeans would fit you, but I might have a pair of old running pants that would stay up."

Nick was skinny. Martin hadn't realized just how thin he was until he'd shown up last night with no shirt on and his pjs plastered to his skin. Nick opened his mouth—likely to argue or tell Martin off, if the look on his face was anything to go by—but Martin forestalled him by turning away and heading to his bedroom.

NICK - FRIDAY

*Fact: Every so often (geologic time), the earth's magnetic poles reverse.
The north pole and the south pole swap magnetism. Scientists estimate
this could happen again about 1000-2000 years from now.*

Probably around the same time Nick Waugh's attitude changes.

Nick made sure Martin knew he didn't *want* to wear Martin's
borrowed clothing. It was that he *had* to. Because he literally
had nothing else to wear. The stretchy black running pants he'd
been lent only stayed up because they had an elastic waist he
could tighten and then fold over. Nick didn't usually feel small;
however, not only was Martin jacked, but Nick had lost a lot of
his muscle mass since his injury.

He didn't *like* feeling like a kid around Martin Purdy. He
didn't *like* the way Martin made him feel *at all*. He *really* didn't
like that Martin made him feel safe. And he hated how hard it
had been last night for him *not* to crawl under the covers with
Martin Purdy like a frightened child.

Last night had scared him more than he wanted to admit. He
was aware enough to admit that—to himself. Screw the gunshot

wound and nightmares from that FUBAR situation, he could have been killed by a fucking rando tree. Which, in the scheme of things, would have just been his luck.

Death by Pinaceae-cide. But he'd saved the cat. Or she had saved him. If Kitten hadn't jumped on him when she did, digging her sharp tiny claws into his skin, Nick might not have woken up. Worried Kitten needed something, he'd grabbed at her, and the next thing he knew, the cabin was exploding around him. It had sounded like a bomb going off.

But he hadn't died in his sleep and he hadn't let go of the cat. Once he'd realized what had happened—that no, an airplane hadn't crashed into his home—Nick had stumbled out of the debris in the only direction he'd known to go. Martin. Like a damn homing pigeon.

And Martin had been kind and had taken him, and the unauthorized feline, in. Even made sure they both warmed up properly. He'd been nice, even when Nick had made it clear he didn't want or need *nice*.

Fuck. Fuck. Fuck.

"Fuck," Nick said out loud.

Martin's arms were crossed over his chest. "Fuck," he agreed, with no idea that Nick was not referring to the damage they were assessing.

To Nick's untrained eye, the destruction looked pretty bad. The massive fir tree hadn't come down directly on the little house. If that had happened, he and Kitten really would be dead. Instead, the tree had fallen at an angle, landing with the trunk pointing northeast toward town. It was the midsize middle limbs that had caught the cabin roof, crushing that corner.

It wasn't a total loss, but the bathroom and living room area would need to be rebuilt. Along with the roof. Okay, which, to be fair, was most of the cabin. Luckily, the mushroom-penis had survived. A phallic beacon.

"You're a damn lucky man, Waugh," Martin said grimly.

"I don't feel lucky."

"You're alive, aren't you?" Martin pointed out.

Nick shrugged. He was still jobless and now homeless again. Nope, not that lucky.

"I guess the thing to do," Martin said, digging into his coat pocket and pulling out a pair of thick work gloves, "is grab what we can of yours and cart it back to my place to dry out. Then I'll see about getting the cabin covered with a tarp. Sorry." He turned to Nick, his brows drawn together as he pulled on the gloves. "There's no way for you to stay here until repairs are finished."

Nick had already reached that depressing conclusion. He was just lucky—that damn word again—he'd stored his laptop and the cameras he never used anymore in a waterproof go bag. As if he'd known something like this might happen. He hadn't, of course, but he always stored his stuff in a waterproof case. When a person traveled as much as he did, *as he had*, it paid to be prepared.

"The other cabins are in much worse shape than this one was, you know that, right?"

Nick eyed Martin.

"Yeah."

"You can't stay in any of them either. They're not livable, not safe."

Nick eyed the row of cabins. Surely one of the ten remaining empty cabins could shelter him? He wasn't picky. After all, he'd spent more than one rainy season trekking in Thailand and ending up with rotten boots and nasty blisters, sleeping in huts, on the beaches, and in trees. He'd volunteered in Sri Lanka, staying in hostels with no walls, only palm-thatched roofs. And a lot of bugs.

But here in Cooper Springs, it was winter and there was just the tiny fact that the electricity to the cabins had been turned off for safety reasons. There was running water but no way to stay warm or to cook. Two of the cabins needed new flooring, and they all needed new roofs, and his had just been added to the list.

"Whatever you're thinking? Absolutely not," Martin said adamantly.

Nick ignored him. He could probably make do. All he needed were some camping supplies. Liam probably had something he could borrow. Incredibly, the little lean-to where he stored his chainsaw and carvings was undamaged. He'd stashed a small camp stove inside as well after picking it up for a few dollars, thinking it might come in handy.

"I could—"

"No. You can't." Martin's expression was grim as he shook his head. "It's not safe," he repeated. "And if I discover you staying in one of those with a camp stove, I will evict you and keep your cat. I know you, er, the Davieses paid you with a roof over your head, and you're welcome to stay with me so I can keep up my end of the bargain I agreed to when I purchased. It's damn small, but we'll manage."

How had Martin known he had a stove? Nick opened his mouth to accuse him of sneaking around his stuff but snapped it shut again when he spotted the stove's dark green lid from where they were standing.

Martin was right, and Nick knew it. It was dangerous to use a propane cooker without proper ventilation, but Martin's promise to evict him sparked his latent anger again.

"Fuck you and the horse you rode in on. I don't need charity from you."

As much as Nick hated it, he was going to have to ask Liam if he could crash at his place until his little cabin was back in shape.

"I'll find somewhere to stay. One of my friends will have space."

Martin's expression told him he had a hard time believing

Nick had any friends in town. Even if it pissed him off, Martin wasn't exactly wrong. Nick had one real friend and one real friend only. If Liam couldn't help him, he was fucked.

"You ask around and let me know," Martin said grimly, wrenching a long bough aside. "Let's get started."

Even with rain still falling, and the wind generally trying to subvert all the work they were doing, it took them less than an hour to retrieve what could be salvaged of Nick's over to Martin's cabin.

Nick stared gloomily down at the pathetic pile of belongings on the living room floor—half of which was cat supplies he'd bought when Xavier drove him to Aberdeen. His gear and laptop—totally fine. His clothing, not that he'd had a lot to start with, was soaking wet and embedded with dirt and pine needles. He nudged the pile with his toe. Nothing else in the cabin was worth saving. The few paperbacks he'd had were spongy masses; they could go in the skip Martin was having delivered.

His clothes probably weren't worth saving either, but Nick didn't have a choice. Thankfully, Martin had a one-piece washer and dryer tucked in next to the bathroom. His first load was already agitating in the washing machine.

Together, they'd managed to wrangle a blue tarp over what was left of the roof, so not much more rainwater was getting inside. Nick had used his chainsaw to cut the smaller tree limbs out of the way, but they were going to need a bigger one for the rest. And, if the burr and rumble of chainsaws coming from across town was any indication, Martin and Nick weren't the only ones who'd woken up to damage.

"At least there's firewood," Martin had grumbled as he pulled the largest limbs away from the structure.

Now Martin was out front, talking to someone. Nick could only hear his voice, so he assumed Martin was on the phone. Hitching Martin's running pants up for the fiftieth time that morning, he headed back outside, passing by Martin without saying anything. He needed to talk to Liam, and sooner rather than later.

"Excuse me, what?" Nick repeated, thinking he hadn't heard correctly the first time.

Liam shook his head again, his expression regretful but resigned. "There's water in the auto shop. Silas is staying on my couch until he can get it sorted out, and I think he's allergic to cats, too. Maybe Magnus can put you up? Or, I dunno, Forrest?"

Nick knew he shouldn't have mentioned the cat.

Liam's cottage had one bedroom and what he jokingly called a bonus room. The bedroom was so small that Liam's mattress touched three walls, and the bonus room was filled with his chainsaws and whatnot. Nick had figured he could crash on his couch. Or the floor.

But, dammit, the resort wasn't the only property with damage. The chorus of chainsaws revving was almost a cacophony and had come at Nick from all directions as he'd walked to Liam's house.

"Why can't you stay at Purdy's?" Liam wanted to know. "You already live there."

Nick clenched his jaw and counted to thirty before answering.

"The other cabins are worse off than mine."

"Not Purdy's though, am I right?"

"No." Nick forced the words out. "His place is fine."

"So? Did he offer you a place to stay?"

Fucking Liam. Why was he Nick's best friend anyway?

"He did offer, but I don't want to stay there. Plus, his couch is really small." That last part made him sound petty. It made him feel petty. Fuck.

"Dude." Liam was shaking his head again. "I'm gonna say this in the nicest way possible, okay?"

A bit apprehensively, Nick nodded.

"Quit being an asshole."

Nick opened his mouth to protest, but Liam held up his hand to stop him from speaking.

"Quit being *that guy* who won't accept a glass of water if he's thirsty. Let some people in, people other than me," Liam clarified. "I know you don't believe it, but there are good people in Cooper Springs. People who—if you'd just let them—want to be your friend." Liam paused and one eye narrowed. "Okay, maybe not right away because you're a prickly asshole, but eventually they'll want to be your friend. And rescuing a kitten does give you points, but the cat probably has the same attitude as you do."

"I think there's more to that water metaphor you used," Nick said bitterly. "A desert or something." Completely ignoring the truths Liam was pointing out.

"It's okay to accept help."

"He didn't offer help. He basically ordered me to accept it."

Liam glanced up at the ceiling for a second and then back at Nick. "Purdy is *offering*. Probably because he feels bad about the tree and is nearly as shook up as you are. I'm pretty sure he's glad you weren't squished. Maybe quit focusing on negatives? I know it's hard when life keeps knocking you down. Can you think of something that made you happy, see if you can expand it to the rest of your life? I know you, Nick. I know who you are under all this bitterness. What was the last thing that made you feel good?"

Trust Liam not to let Nick get away with being pissed off and mad—even though he had every right to be. Also trust him to remember Nick's rant about the therapist.

Thankfully, Nick was not the sort who blushed. But he still couldn't look Liam in the eye as the memory of Martin making him tea in his kitchen surged back. It had been such a normal, *nice* gesture, one any normal person would have done. It had literally made his heart clench. His parents hadn't physically abused him, but they had put a price on their affection.

And yeah, he knew that what they thought was parental love was in fact something so fucked up he didn't know what to call it. They'd locked him out of the house because they "loved" him enough to teach him a lesson. Probably they'd say the tree falling last night was another "love" lesson.

Grabbing his shoulders, Liam pulled Nick close and wrapped his arms around him in a bear hug, squeezing the air out of Nick's lungs. Liam was the only person Nick allowed this sort of behavior from. After what seemed like an excessive period of time, Liam released him and stepped away.

"What was that for?" Nick complained.

"Because you needed it."

Nick was saved from having to search for a caustic reply by a knock on Liam's front door.

"Come on in," Liam called out.

The door opened and Silas Murphy stepped inside. He had a duffle bag over one shoulder and was carrying a cardboard box.

A thought struck Nick. "Don't you live *over* the auto shop?" he asked.

Silas nodded. "Not anymore. Not until I can get the roof fixed."

"Fuck." Nick glanced at Liam, who was definitely giving him a side-eye. Oh, right, Silas needed sympathy too. "Er. That sucks. Hopefully, it'll get taken care of soon. I have a feeling carpenters are going to be in high demand around here."

"Yeah," Silas said quietly, setting the box down on the coffee table and the duffle bag on the floor.

Nick thought Silas was a few years older than Liam and he were, but he was one of those guys where it was hard to tell his age. He was tall and wiry, with dark hair that showed a bit of gray at the temples. It also looked as if Silas possibly cut it himself. Liam had told him that Silas had inherited the auto shop when his dad passed away a few years ago.

"A tree fell on Nick's place last night," Liam informed him.

Silas's gaze swung to Nick for just a second. "Oh, no, that's terrible."

"It didn't fall on me, just close enough to do some damage."

"I'm glad you weren't hurt." Silas glanced over at Liam and then back at Nick. "Do you need a place to stay? I could probably crash somewhere else."

That was the second longest set of sentences Silas had ever spoken to Nick. And damn if he didn't feel guilty for really wishing Silas would give up the couch even though he knew Liam wouldn't allow it. Liam's green gaze was focused on Nick with unpleasant intensity.

"Nope. I'm good. Mar–er, Purdy offered me a spot on his couch."

"Okay. That's good," Silas said with evident relief. "But, you know, if something changes, let me or Liam know."

"Sure thing." He jabbed his thumb over his shoulder. "I should get back to helping Purdy clean up."

Liam clapped him on the back. "Everything is gonna work out, I promise."

Nick rolled his eyes; Liam's sunny optimism was hard to take on the best days, and today was not one of those.

"I'll talk to you later."

The mile-long walk back home felt to Nick like some kind of kinky walk of shame, and every ten feet he had to hitch up the borrowed running pants. Nick didn't want to apologize or be nice; he just wanted to *be*. Instead, he was going to have to do both: apologize and be nice. The fucking world was coming to an end.

. . .

Martin and Magnus, of all people, were busy cutting up the tree trunk when Nick returned from Liam's. In truth, Rufus was supervising while Magnus and Martin did the work. Nick spotted Wanda Stone coming from the other direction, carrying a thermos and a small cooler. The town was out helping each other.

That was nice, he grudgingly supposed. Happy thoughts, bah.

Spotting Nick, Magnus cut the saw's motor, setting it down on the thick tree trunk.

"Nick, you are one lucky bastard."

"Keep telling me and I might start to believe it one day."

Magnus stared at him, his eyebrows rising almost to his hairline. "You survived being shot. Now you've survived a tree falling literally feet from where you were sleeping. You are damn lucky. You're going to have townsfolk lining up to walk across the street next to you."

"Lucky would have been not being in the line of fire in the first place," Nick argued. There was nothing lucky at all about a gunshot wound.

"Nope," Magnus disagreed. Martin stood next to Magnus, an amused expression on his face, as if he knew exactly what was going through Nick's head. Which was impossible because Martin hardly knew Nick. "Nope," Magnus repeated. "You're just thinking about things all backward." Reaching out a long arm, Magnus clapped Nick on the shoulder hard enough he had to take a step forward or risk falling on his face. "You'll figure it out."

"What is today?" Nick wondered aloud. "National Improve Nick Waugh Day?"

"That would be an international holiday," Martin muttered. Magnus snorted.

Gaping at his landlord for a hot second, Nick lifted one hand

and raised his middle finger in both men's direction. It was meant in a friendly sort of way. Kind of.

Hours later, they'd finished cleaning up what they could. There was now a stack of firewood that would get Martin through several chilly winters. Magnus, Rufus, and Wanda had moved on to the next towny who needed hot coffee, snacks, and a big-ass chainsaw to get through the day. Nick heard that Vincent Barone was working his magic on the other end of town, along with Xavier, Liam probably had joined them.

Exhausted and irritated, Nick followed Martin back to his place and into his tiny kitchen, where Martin made tea for them both. Kitten—he needed a name for her—mewed and hopped down off the couch at the sight of him. Nick scooped her up and cuddled her little body. Martin said nothing about Nick staying somewhere else. Nick was thankful for that; he didn't think he could handle outright kindness from his landlord. Acceptance of his presence was all he needed.

"Sorry for being a dick earlier," Nick said finally, hoping Martin understood that "earlier" meant *all* the times Nick had been a jerk.

Martin nodded. "No offense taken."

The clothes he'd had to wash were clean and dry now. Nick grabbed out some jeans, a t-shirt, and underwear, taking them with him to change in the bathroom while Martin made dinner and muttered something about needing carbs. Folding up the track pants, Nick tiptoed into Martin's bedroom and set them on top of the colorful comforter spread across the mattress. Martin was obviously the kind of person who made his bed every morning regardless of circumstances.

The mattress was huge and took up all the room except for a few feet at the end along one side. It was one of those kings with extra inches, and Martin was right. It was big enough for both of them. But no way was he sharing Martin's bed. No matter how much he wanted to.

No way. Not going to happen.

He'd get an air mattress and sleep on the living room floor before he'd share with Martin Purdy. Something told him if he caved on this point, the rest of his protests about Martin would fall like dominoes.

Martin called out, "Do you have any allergies?"

"No," Nick answered, irrationally irritated—again—that Martin was thoughtful.

"You like crime shows?" Martin asked randomly. "When I'm kind of wound up, I like to watch old episodes of *Law and Order.* Wouldn't mind watching a few tonight."

MARTIN - TWO WEEKS LATER

Fact: Metamorphic rocks always begin as another type of rock. Metamorphic literally means changed form.

"Excuse me, what?"

"A tree fell on Nick's cabin," Martin repeated, even though he knew Simon had heard him perfectly well the first time. "He's staying with me until we can get it repaired."

There was a very loud silence on the other end of the line.

"The murderous chainsaw guy is staying in your house *—while you sleep?*"

This was why Martin had waited a few days—fourteen of them, to be exact—to actually call Simon.

"What was I going to do, Simon? Kick him out? The cabin was his home, and I agreed to let him live there for the duration of the Davies agreement."

The man in question had showered and left the cabin midmorning. Martin didn't know what he was doing, and it wasn't Martin's business where Nick went. Martin was not his parent and barely his roommate. The fact that Nick had starred in several of Martin's recent dreams without his permission was a nuance that just added to all the weirdness—and indicated that, regardless of their age difference, *parental* was not the direction Martin's feelings for Nick were headed.

"The hell." Simon's voice rose. "Does he not have friends he can stay with? He doesn't have any, does he? And you know why, Martin? Because he's an asshole."

While Simon was ranting, Martin took a deep breath in through his nose, held it for a moment, then released it. As he counted to ten, he also vowed not to let on that he was very much attracted to Nick.

"He… can be a bit rough but he's not an asshole, and he does have friends but—really, Simon, I don't need to justify my actions to you. And you, of all people, know I'm not the type to refuse to help someone who needs it." And Nick had rescued a kitten, which made him a hero in some circles.

"I know, I know." Simon sighed, probably remembering how Martin had helped him out when he was a young doctoral student. "I just don't want him taking advantage of you."

Martin smiled. It was nice knowing someone had his back, even if he lived miles away.

"Sleeping on the floor is not taking advantage, believe me."

Maybe Nick was going to Aberdeen to see a massage therapist. If Martin had slept on that camping pad for two weeks, he'd be needing surgery by now.

"I suppose it's not," he conceded. "I warned you that couch was too short. How long?"

Martin decided Simon was asking how long until repairs were finished, not the couch's dimensions.

"The guys I hired are hoping to come out before the holiday, but they're not making any promises. In the meantime, I've pulled out the cabinets and counters. It's all going to have to be redone. Luckily, the rest of the cabins weren't damaged any further. And the new windows are on schedule for January, maybe even next week."

"That's not what I meant, and you know it. How long are you going to let him freeload? Is he going to pay you with pornographic chainsaw art?"

Martin laughed, glad he hadn't told Simon about the penises. "Maybe he is. But he hasn't been doing much of that recently. He's actually been helping me out."

Nick had helped Martin unpack the rest of his boxes and figure out where to put all of his things. Martin suspected it was because Nick didn't want to trip on them, but then, neither did Martin.

He'd gone on to hang the flat-screen TV above the fireplace across from the too-short couch. They'd celebrated by spending a few evenings watching *Law and Order*, *CSI*, then the new *Reacher*. Nick was under the false impression that *CSI: Vegas* was the best of the lot. Martin would change his mind soon enough.

The artwork Martin had deemed worthy of his new home was now hanging on the walls—even if it would have to come down when he decided on an interior color. Even better (or worse, although Martin wasn't embarrassed to admit his phobia, everyone should be afraid of spiders), an early morning arachnid encounter in the kitchen meant Nick discovering Martin's fear of spiders.

"It's just a tiny spider!" Nick exclaimed while Martin bravely attempted not to cower. It was all he could do not to grab a rubber spatula off the counter and smash it to smithereens. Then burn the spatula.

"I don't care if it's a little old granny spider who sits in her spider rocking chair knitting little baby spider hats." Martin pointed at it. "It's got to go."

Laughing, Nick scooped it up—with his bare hand!—and tossed it outside. "You're gonna feel bad when you find Granny

Spider curled up in a little ball and dead," he said when he came back inside.

"No, I will not. I will rejoice."

"That's a bit harsh." But Nick said it with a smile, and Martin counted it as a win.

Thus, Nick had been the one to empty out the shed. And then he refilled it with the knickknacks Martin was saving for the cabins and which were also now packed safely inside secure plastic containers to keep them from getting damp.

"Huh," Simon said, bringing Martin back to the present.

"*Huh* all you want. I only called to keep you up-to-date."

"I hate to admit it, but you sound happy."

"I am happy," Martin assured him. Even if he was plagued by unasked-for erections and the damn dreams that put his and Joe's sex life to shame. Nothing he needed to share with Simon.

"I suppose that's something."

Martin heard a noise in the background, maybe a door opening and closing.

"Charley's home," Simon informed him. He heard some hushed muttering and a sigh. "I have to go. Apparently, we're going tree shopping, or some such nonsense."

Simon might complain, but Martin knew he loved Charley and would go tree shopping for days if that's what Charley wanted to do. Martin wasn't exactly jealous, but sometimes he had little twinges that he might be missing out on something. His newly awakened cock was not helping.

"Have fun. I'll keep you in my thoughts," Martin promised. "Glad I'm not being dragged all over the city looking for the perfect tree."

"There will be drinking afterward, so there's that."

"I'll raise a pint for you, then."

Since he'd basically promised Simon he'd have a drink in his honor, Martin decided to head over to the Steam Donkey. The pub was technically in walking distance, but he drove anyway.

Rain was pelting down without any sign of it letting up soon or even in the next week, and he really didn't feel like putting on his rain gear yet again.

It was one of those December days when the sun never seemed to fully rise. These short winter days had never been Martin's favorites no matter where he lived, and he was looking forward to them getting longer again.

While he'd been unpacking, organizing, and working on the cabins, Cooper Springs had festooned itself in holiday decorations. And, like a very prickly personal TV newscaster, Nick kept him up-to-date with a nightly report about each new hideous display as it went up.

"It's like there's a competition to be awful," Nick had said one evening as he stood at the front window. "I do not remember this about Cooper Springs. Did I miss it when I was a kid? Was I just that oblivious?"

Martin silently agreed the decorations were awful, but he also felt guilty having disparaging thoughts about his new town.

"Kids growing up here are going to have PTSD from seeing Santa falling off roofs and hanging onto gutters by his fingertips. And what's with the one with Lady Claus and, like, seven Santas? Is that a harem?" Nick had turned to Martin, who stood next to him nursing a mug of orange spice tea. "It *is*, isn't it? A reverse harem with *Santas*."

"I think...." Martin managed after he stopped coughing, "they're supposed to be elves."

"Still could be a harem," Nick pointed out.

When Martin pushed inside the pub, the first thing he heard was Magnus's booming laugh. This was followed by the realization that *She's Like the Wind* from *Dirty Dancing* was playing overhead. The fact that Martin recognized the song was personally embarrassing. He'd gone through a Patrick Swayze stage when he'd been a teen. He'd had the movie poster and the movie's soundtrack, which his dad had finally banned him from playing when his parents were home.

Realizing he was gay—by Martin, his parents, and even his Aunt Heidi—had quickly followed. Tragically, Patrick had never responded to any of Martin's fan letters.

Critter was sitting next to Rufus, Magnus stood behind the bar, and they were all looking at something on Critter's phone. Martin took the empty spot on the other side of Critter and peered over to see what they were looking at.

"They let *you* be in charge?" Magnus wheezed. "Who the hell came up with that idea?"

"I kinda took it upon myself since no one else was doing it," Critter responded. "Mags has been helping."

"Of course she has," Magnus said. "She's probably the brains behind all of it. Although I have my doubts about this one."

Nick was nowhere in sight. Martin hadn't expected to see him but still wondered what he was up to. With no car, he couldn't have gone far.

"What's going on?" Martin asked.

"Critter's put himself in charge of social media for the forest," Rufus said. "Go on, show him."

Critter turned his phone around so Martin could see the screen.

"I'm just promoting our part of the park, of course. I came up with this one myself."

One of these cougars is dangerous—know your wildlife.

Below that was a picture of a fierce-looking cougar next to a head shot of an older White woman. The pictures were followed by wild animal safety tips, one of which was—*please don't mess with the wildlife.*

"Eight thousand views?" Martin said. "Holy cow."

He wanted to know who the woman was; glancing up from the phone, he caught Magnus's smirk.

Critter nodded. "We're kind of in a feud with the National Park Service. They think they're so funny. But they're not." He pointed his thumb at his chest. "We're the funny ones."

"Huh," said Martin. Realizing he sounded a lot like Simon, he added, "that's… great. I didn't know we had cougars here."

Rufus snorted and Magnus guffawed.

"Not down here, of course," Critter agreed. "They tend to live higher up. But sometimes, if they're hungry, they'll come down for a meal."

"Um, wondering. Who's the woman?" And did Critter have her permission to make fun of her?

"My older sister."

Magnus and Rufus snorted in tandem. Martin eyed the Forest Service officer; did he have a death wish? Critter wasn't paying attention to their reactions because he was too busy refreshing his feed, presumably to see how many new likes and shares he had.

"I think," Magnus said, breaking the silence, "that Critter is getting back at Lael for something she did to him when he was eight."

"I'm not!" Critter protested. "This stuff is funny." He checked the post again. "We're getting tons of likes. We're going to be famous."

"Famous for being ax-murdered by your sister," Magnus said.

"Lael won't see it. She's never on social media."

Magnus and Rufus both gave Critter looks that told Martin that Critter was probably very wrong about his sister's social media habits.

"She is going to kill you when she finds out." Magnus shook his head. "I went to school at the same time as Lael. She was a few years ahead of me," he said to Martin. "Lael was a person you didn't cross."

"Try living in the same house with her," Critter muttered. "I was never happier than when she graduated and went off to college."

Magnus nodded, apparently in agreement with Critter.

"Where does she live?" Martin asked. Maybe she didn't live in Cooper Springs.

"Over by the mansion, thereabouts," Critter said, staring at his phone again.

Rufus sat back, crossing his arms over his chest. "You are an idiot. Did Mags sign off on this one?"

"Nah, she said I should just run with it."

"I don't think she meant like this," Magnus muttered. "This here is more of a 'how fast can you run away' situation."

The front door burst open. Martin twisted around and watched as an older person stumbled inside. He'd sort of expected to see Critter's sister, but all Martin was certain of was that the newcomer was a human senior citizen. They had Einstein-gray hair, which appeared to have been ravaged by the wind and rain into a standing tornado. Their clothes were baggy and ultimately shapeless, making it impossible for Martin to even hazard a guess.

"I saw him. Rufus, *I saw him.*" The voice was raspy, like they had a ten-pack-a-day habit.

Rufus was immediately on his feet, his expression gleeful. Critter and his tweets, forgotten.

"You did? Come, have a seat and tell me all about it."

Martin wondered who Rufus and the stranger were referring to. They'd said *he* so all he knew was it hadn't been Critter's older sister.

"Magnus, a lemonade, please," Rufus called to his son.

With an infinitesimal shake of the head, Magnus bent down to open the undercounter fridge. Out the side of his mouth, he muttered, "Sasquatch," clearing up Martin's confusion.

"Who is this?" Martin quietly asked Critter.

"What?" Raising his head, Critter looked around. He'd been

so intent on his phone again that he hadn't realized someone had joined them. "Ah, Oliver Cox. He runs the post office and is in charge of the mail delivery around here, such as it is."

"I saw him," Cox declared again. "I saw him with my own eyes."

"Calm down, Ollie," Rufus said. "When you're ready, I want to hear every detail."

A battered notebook appeared in Rufus's hand, presumably pulled out from the front pocket of the plaid padded jacket he wore, and a pen, too. He was prepared to record the details of what Martin suspected was a Sasquatch sighting. Even Critter stopped monitoring his rising fame.

Stopping in front of him, Magnus said, "Sorry, Martin, I was a bit distracted there. Can I pour you a beer?"

Martin eyed the colorful tap handles. "I'll have a Rainy Day Pale, please."

A minute later, Magnus set the beer in front of him. "How's the tarp holding up on Five?" He asked.

"Fine." Martin waggled his head. "Kinda wish we could do more work on it, but it's touch and go in this weather."

Magnus leaned a hip against the bar, clearly intending to chat for a few minutes and not interested in the Bigfoot retelling happening a few feet away.

"Nice of you to let Nick stay with you."

Martin waved off the compliment. "Anybody would've done it."

"Not so sure about that," Magnus teased. His bushy eyebrows waggled, resembling caterpillars on steroids. "Our Nick can be a handful, but just ignore the sharpness and bluster."

"Eh, it's growing on me. Nick's a good person." His eyes met Magnus's thoughtful gaze and Martin thought he saw some sort of satisfaction, or maybe it was an approval of Martin's reply. It seemed he'd answered correctly and passed a test he didn't know about? "Anyway," he continued, "any news about the missing girl? Blair Cruz, right?"

A gusty sigh escaped Magnus as he straightened up from the bar. "No." He shook his head. "Nothing. Poor Levi is losing his mind."

"I don't think I've met Levi."

"Aye, likely not. Vincent says he's staying at home by the phone."

"Hasn't it been around a month now?"

"Aye, it has," Magnus nodded. "A month, and no hint of a sign at all. And after Lizzie, too," he said as he nodded his chin in the direction of the beach. "He's beside himself with worry. Blaming himself for all manner of things. Not paying attention —so Blair could do whatever she wanted. Paying too much attention—so Blair felt stifled. Missing signs of unhappiness. At least this is what Vincent says."

"Vincent—Xavier Stone's Vincent?" Martin did an inner fist bump at getting the name and partner correct.

Magnus nodded, his attention shifting back to the mail carrier and Rufus.

Martin eyed Oliver Cox. He was one of those people who could be fifty or eighty. Tall and skinny to the point of cadaverousness—was that a word?—he'd clearly spent a lot of his life out of doors. His cheeks were leathery and deeply lined, and everything about him was long. Long fingers—slowly moving in front of him as he told his story—long nose, narrow head.

He reminded Martin of a stick bug. And it didn't help that Cox's jacket and heavy pants were army green.

Martin remembered that Xavier had told him Rufus was the President of the local Bigfoot Society. At the time, Martin had inwardly scoffed, but now... it was clear that Rufus Ferguson took sightings of the creature very seriously.

Cox sipped at the lemonade, continuing to hold the glass in his hand while he related what he'd supposedly seen. Martin only half paid attention as he wasn't a believer. Yes, there were as yet uncontacted tribes in the Amazon rainforest, but not on the Olympic Peninsula, just over one hundred miles from Seattle.

Did he believe that *humans* probably lived in the forests and on other public land? Yes. And not humans like the Quinault, Hoh, and Quileute tribal members, who had legal access to the forest land as well as protected sacred areas where not even the likes of Critter and Mags were allowed unless invited.

Martin dismissed the newcomer. Instead, he sipped his beer and half-listened to the *Dirty Dancing* soundtrack which—tragically—had been permanently embedded in his memory. He supposed there were worse things than knowing the words to every single lyric. He was humming along with *Some Kind of Wonderful* when Nick wandered in and claimed the seat next to him.

"Sasquatch sighting?" Nick asked.

He must have been carving because he smelled like rain and freshly cut wood. Since it was raining, Martin was going to assume he'd been working somewhere covered.

Martin nodded. "How did you know?" He shifted in his seat, and his cock twitched. The scent of woodchips and sawdust was quickly becoming some sort of weird Nick-related turn-on.

"Cox is one of the regulars."

Martin eyed Nick for a second. He had a smirky, knowing expression on his handsome face. The penny dropped.

"Oh, you mean he sees them all the time?"

"Yup." Nick nodded.

"Check it out, Nick," Critter interjected. He shoved his phone past Martin so Nick could see the screen. "I'm famous."

"What am I looking at?" Nick asked.

"Apparently the human-cougar is Critter's sister," Martin muttered.

Nick snorted. "This is your sister? Dude, you are a dead man."

"That's what I said—basically." Magnus had abandoned the Sasquatch report and wandered over to their corner of the bar. "Lael is going to end you when she finds out."

The door opened for a third—or was it fourth?—time and they all automatically looked to see who was coming inside. Except for Critter, who returned to monitoring his likes and shares.

"And maybe sooner, rather than later," Magnus added.

NICK

Fact: The oldest minerals from Earth's crust discovered to date are the zircons found in Archean metamorphosed sedimentary rock from the Jack Hills of southwestern Australia.

"Well," Nick said as he slid into the passenger seat next to Martin. "That was more fun than I expected today."

Normally he'd have walked back to the cabins, but it was pissing down hard, so he figured he might as well accept a ride from Martin. He just wasn't going to let himself get used to it.

"I feel a little bit sorry for Critter," Martin said as he started his car.

"He brought it on himself," Nick pointed out. "Although Lael is probably lucky. Seeing as she didn't get hauled away for assault."

The police hadn't been forced to intervene, although Magnus had threatened to call them when Critter's sister—who was close to sixty but kept herself in excellent shape—began beating on Critter's back with her fists and kicking at his chair. And screaming. The screaming had been a bit much. After Magnus and Rufus had calmed her down, they all watched as Critter reluctantly deleted the post, cutting short his rise to fame.

"Are you doing anything for the holiday?" Martin asked out of the blue.

"Wha—oh, Christmas? No. Why?" Nick narrowed his eyes, watching the wipers flip back and forth, chasing raindrops across the windshield. "Are you going somewhere? Family coming to visit or something? You want me to find somewhere else to stay?"

"No, I don't want, or need, you to find somewhere else. I was just asking, making conversation. My parents are dead and no, I'm not going anywhere."

"Oh." Nick felt the slightest bit foolish. "Uh, that's good. Good to know." Oh, shit. He squeezed his eyes shut. "Uh, not that your parents are dead. I didn't mean that."

Martin chuckled. "I figured not."

They passed the Pizza Mart with its disturbing neon Santa glowing in the front window. Nick thought it was supposed to be tossing pizza dough, but that part had burned out so the Santa just kept bending down and straightening up for no apparent reason. Maybe he was giving one of the elves a blow job? Nobody ever accused Nick of not having a good imagination.

"When is it, anyway?" Since he didn't care about the upcoming holiday, he had no idea when it happened other than soon. Half the time, he didn't know what day it was.

"Monday."

Nick's curiosity got the better of him. "What are you going to do?" He didn't have the impression that Martin celebrated, but what did he know?

"Sleep in. Drink coffee. Get a roaring fire going in the fireplace. Finish the mystery I'm reading. If you're up for it, we can try and find some truly horrible TV. That's kind of a Christmas tradition for me."

"What, like the animated Rudolf or something? Or *He-Man and She-Ra's Christmas Special*—because I can assure you that show was an abomination. They might as well have lit several thousand dollars on fire. I don't even know why Liam and I insisted on watching it."

"Oh, you have so much to learn. That's child's play. I don't mean bad holiday shows, I mean bad TV in general. And after making me watch *CSI: Cyber* the other day, I'm thinking you need to watch *Starsky and Hutch*. The original, not the hideous remake with Ben Stiller. Which, to be fair, qualifies, but even I can't stoop that low."

"*Starsky and Hutch*... is that the one with the woman whose underwear covers more than her shorts?" Nick's tone was innocent, but a quick glance told Martin he was full of crap.

"No, but I'm sure we can arrange some *Dukes of Hazzard*, if that's what you really want. Somebody has to be streaming it."

Martin turned on his indicator, and they headed up the road to the cabins. "Maybe make a nice dinner later in the day. I'm going to Aberdeen for groceries tomorrow. Do you want to join me?"

Nick opened his mouth and then froze. He'd been about to say yes.

What the hell was up with that?

Pulling the car into his regular spot in the parking lot, Martin turned off the engine.

"Nick," Martin said as he turned to look at him, a small smile dancing across his stupidly sexy lips, "you don't have to decide right this minute. It's not as if I'm taking reservations. If you decide you want to go, feel free to join me."

Nick rolled his eyes, making sure Martin didn't miss it.

"Sure, fine. I'll let you know." He probably needed cat food or something.

. . .

Late the next morning, Nick was back in the passenger seat of Martin's car. Currently, they were crossing over the bridge into Aberdeen. Rain continued to fall, and the sun was hidden behind thick clouds. The small city was fighting the gloom as best it could with glittering and flashing holiday lights, enough for a small kingdom.

When Martin had reminded Nick that he was heading out, Nick had just trailed along like—like he'd always been planning on tagging along with him. It made Nick irritable. Martin confused him.

Why would Purdy—*Martin*—want to spend time with Nick when he didn't have to? Nick was merely an interloper, a blip on the other man's radar, and he would soon be gone. Or, not living underfoot all the time.

Martin was obviously a sucker for punishment. That was the only reasonable explanation.

"Do you have anything special you like to cook this time of year?" Martin asked him, oblivious to Nick's inner struggle. Or choosing to ignore it. Nick was beginning to suspect that Martin caught on to more than Nick wanted him to.

"No," Nick said honestly.

Martin started to say something else, but they came over a rise and a billboard with a picture of a missing girl came into view. Not Blair Cruz. This was Angela Wiggen, the girl that had disappeared last summer. The school-style portrait took up one third of the space and the rest was a description of what she'd been wearing and where she'd last been seen. Investigators and her family asked anyone with information to please call a 1-800 number.

"Every time I see that billboard, it makes my stomach hurt. I just can't imagine what the family must be going through," Martin said as they passed it.

"I doubt they have much hope. It's been almost five months."

"I suppose not. Hopefully, things go differently with Blair Cruz. I haven't heard anything, have you?"

Nick shook his head before realizing Martin's focus was on the road. "No, I haven't heard anything."

They were both quiet after that. Nick stared out the window; traffic didn't seem too bad, but his frame of reference was Cooper Springs and its single stoplight. Nick's opinion changed the minute Martin flicked on his turn signal.

"What the fuckery is this?" Nick demanded to know.

The grocery store's parking lot was packed, and drivers were waiting for spaces to open up, stalking shoppers to their spots as they left the store.

"Christmas is in two days, so this is last-minute shopping at its finest."

"Oh, my fucking god." Nick couldn't take his eyes off the teeming mass of people going in and coming back out of the store. More cars were in a line trying to turn into the rows closest to the entrance. Shoppers pushed carts filled to the limit and then some with everything they thought they needed. Was there going to be anything left by the time he and Martin got inside? "It's not Armageddon. The shops will only be closed for one day. This is America—what is *wrong* with people?"

Martin laughed. "Quit grouching and help me find a spot."

He headed to the back of the lot, but it still took ten minutes before they nabbed a spot in one of the last rows. Nick met Martin at the back of his SUV, and they started toward the entrance.

"Are you sure this is worth taking our lives into our hands?" Nick asked as they were nearly mowed down by not one, but two different cars.

"This is nothing. The store in my old neighborhood would have lines around the block just to park. We're not in a hurry. Think of it as an adventure."

"I've had plenty of adventure, thank you very much."

Nick thought—quietly, to himself—that Martin's idea of adventure was twisted. The man actually seemed to enjoy the madness that was the grocery store two days before Christmas.

Once they found a cart, which was like discovering gold, Martin started whistling an aimless tune as he pushed it toward the produce section. As he poked through the piles of potatoes and onions, he started humming along with the cheesy carols playing overhead. In the spice section, he joked as he helped another shopper reach crackers on the top shelf.

Not that Nick wouldn't have helped her too, but joking like old friends was a step too far.

Then there was the checkout line.

"What the actual fuck?"

Martin was deftly maneuvering the cart through the crowds, trying to find the end of the queue.

"This right here is the definition of insanity," Nick said as they finally tucked in behind a young couple with a toddler and a baby. The toddler was loudly complaining to anyone who would listen—because his parents were ignoring him—that he was bored and wanted to go home.

A hand landed on Nick's shoulder. "Do not encourage him," Martin whispered. His lips brushed against the shell of Nick's ear, sending a shock of awareness through his body and directly to his cock.

No, he thought fiercely, *no, no, no. I've already been down this path.* The past month had been a unique form of torture. The cabin was eight hundred square feet. If the wind was quiet, he could hear Martin's shifts in his bed, his light snores, the rustle of the covers. In the dark of night, Nick wanted to be like the traitorous Kitten and just waltz in and curl up next to Martin.

Not just curl up. He wanted to do other things, too. Sleeping on the floor meant he woke with an aching back and a throbbing dick every morning and there was nothing he could do about either of them. Just thinking about it—like right this minute—made his cock stand at attention.

"Fine," Nick said through gritted teeth.

It took them over an hour to check out and it proved impossible for them not to bump into each other as the line moved. A hip. A thigh. Shoulders. Telling himself *no* hadn't worked. By the time they got to the front of the line, Nick was a wreck, with an erection that wouldn't go away. He was just thankful Martin had stepped to the front of the cart to unload it and be fucking nice to the checker.

"You got quiet in there, everything okay?" Martin asked him when they'd made it back through the obstacle course of a parking lot and were loading the groceries into the back of the car.

Nick heaved a particularly heavy bag into the car. "Just... people," was all he could come up with. Martin would not be impressed by him announcing, *I have a massive boner.*

His New Year's resolution was going to be something along the lines of: No obsessing about Martin Purdy. No unnecessary thinking about him. No erections.

That was three, but they all boiled down to the same thing. *No Martin Purdy.*

They were finally at the head of the line to turn out of the parking lot when a flash of black caught Nick's attention. The SUV was driving too fast, weaving around slower-moving vehicles as it headed toward the bridge.

"What the actual fuck?" He jerked forward, peering out the windshield. "It's that same fucking car." He was sure of it.

"What's wrong?" Martin asked.

"Follow that car," Nick demanded, pointing at it. "The black Sequoia, or whatever it is."

A lucky break in traffic allowed Martin to pull out. Quickly, he moved into the same lane as the SUV, but the other car was already cruising through the intersection and the walk-light told Nick the light was about to turn.

"Don't let it get away!" Nick begged. "Keep after it. Goddammit," he groaned as the light turned red. They were trapped on the wrong side of it, stuck behind a minivan with a decal on the back that had Nick thinking the owners needed to consider birth control.

"Fucking hell! Motherfucking cocksuckers got away again!" Nick slapped the dash as he watched the black car get smaller and smaller, crest the rise of the bridge, and disappear altogether.

"Care to explain what that was about?" Martin asked.

Nick collapsed against the seat, crossing his arms over his chest.

"Not really. You wouldn't believe me anyway."

"Try me."

"Fine." He huffed out a breath. "Everyone else thinks I'm crazy, so it won't matter if you get added to the list."

"Nick," Martin said, "just tell me. I'll be the judge of whether I think you've lost your marbles or not. To be fair, not sure how many you were playing with to begin with."

"Fuck off," he said without heat. Another sigh escaped him before he could stop it.

"Quit stalling."

The light turned green. Martin stepped on the gas, and they lurched forward, following the minivan through the intersection and onto the bridge.

"Are there even enough seats in that van for the amount of spawn they claim to have?" Nick wondered, totally stalling.

"Nick," Martin ground out. "The SUV—what about it?"

They'd reached the rise and, as Nick had known, the SUV was nowhere in sight. Just a lot of regular holiday traffic. It could be anywhere but behind them.

"That car's been coming around Cooper Springs." Telling

Martin was like pulling off a Band-Aid, an expected pain. He stared out the window and watched the old fisherman's cottages of Aberdeen slide by as he spoke, not looking at Martin. Seeing the "I'm listening but not hearing you" expression on that face would be too hard. "I'm ninety-nine percent positive it's the same one. I saw it in October, driving too fast down The Strip. Then again, a few days later. Each time I've seen it turn down a different street—I think it has anyway. Why? What are they looking for? All they'd need to do is stop at the pub and ask. No one cares about privacy in town."

He risked a glance at Martin. At the moment, he was focused on the road. But he was also nodding, as if what Nick was saying made complete sense.

"The last time was just before Thanksgiving. I tried to follow it on foot."

"No luck?"

"Nope. All I got was soaking wet."

"Hmm. This car is setting off your Spidey senses?"

Nick narrowed his eyes, but Martin didn't seem to be mocking him. "I suppose that's a good way of putting it."

"Well, I guess we'll both have to start watching. Two pairs of eyes are better than one."

"You really believe me?"

Martin quickly glanced at him and then back at the road. "Why wouldn't I?"

"Probably because you don't know me very well. Everybody I've mentioned it to thinks I'm being paranoid. Even Liam. Although last time he said I should tell the cops. As if they'd listen."

"I know you plenty well, Nick. Maybe not as well as Liam does. But I have a pretty good handle on who you are, and therefore, yes, I believe you."

Nick gaped at Martin for a few seconds before snapping his mouth shut.

"We'll both keep our eyes open," Martin continued. "If we have any luck at all, we'll figure out what they're up to—maybe it's something harmless, but what you've told me definitely seems weird." He paused for a second. "Just so you know, for this scenario, I'm Hutch and you're Starsky."

"What? No!" Nick protested. "Starsky flies off the handle all the time." He scowled. "Just... *no*. Why are we even talking about this? They aren't real. They're made up!"

MARTIN - NEW YEARS EVE

Fact: Geologic time began ticking when Earth formed, approximately 4.6 billion years ago. To fit this large amount of time relative to the Gregorian calendar year, each of the 12 months of the geologic calendar year represents 383 million years. Martin Purdy has lived 42 of those years or 15,330 days. Thirty-three or so of those days in the same space as Nick Waugh.

The new year would begin in about an hour. Martin had bundled himself up in his parka, scarf, knit cap, jeans, thick wool socks, and tall boots. Then, he'd followed the path that started at his door and led to the top of the bluff overlooking the beach and the ocean.

From there, he planned on enjoying the random fireworks being set off along the stretch of sandy beach. The moon was almost full, its soft light illuminating the hilltop and the scene below. Martin could just barely make out tiny figures spread out along the beach, many with flashlights, staking out their firework setting-off territory.

Totally illegal, of course, but if someone was going to set them off, Martin was going to enjoy them.

He'd been invited to join in the celebration by both Magnus and Xavier, separately, but he'd politely declined, wanting to greet January 1 on his own terms. He was definitely feeling thoughtful this year. A large crowd didn't appeal.

Hunkering down on this two-hundred-foot-high bluff that protected Cooper Springs from the Pacific Ocean was diametrically different from his old life. In the past, he'd either made the trek to a local park and celebrated with hundreds of people he didn't know or just stayed home and watched the ball drop on TV.

This was better. So much better. That same little *click* inside himself when he'd seen the resort for the first time repeated itself. As if his soul was releasing a satisfied sigh.

The last month had been challenging, and even frustrating, at times. And every damn morning, Martin had woken with morning wood that was becoming harder and harder to ignore. So far, he *had* managed to disregard it, but one of these days he was going to crack—hopefully when Nick was out of the house. However, aside from the sexual frustration, the past weeks had also been surprisingly satisfying. The puzzle that was Nick Waugh was slowly revealing itself.

He was still sleeping on Martin's living room floor—the couch had won that round. Nick's—and Kitten's—continued presence was a daily reminder that work on the cabins wasn't going as quickly as he'd thought it would. But wasn't that always the case with construction, especially around the holidays? And Nick Waugh, a man Martin had originally seen as an obstacle and irritant, was slowly morphing into an *almost* friend. Even if sometimes Martin's patience was tested.

This morning was a perfect example. Martin returned from his weekly trip to Aberdeen to find not one, not two, but *three* more of the odd penis carvings sitting smack dab in the middle of the lawn in front of the cabins. It had been the first time he'd seen any since he'd threatened to burn that first one.

Martin was certain Nick resented their enforced intimacy, but they'd gotten to know each other, regardless. It was impossible not to while sharing a seven-hundred-and-ninety-six square-foot living space. Maybe the penises were his way of protesting? Who knew?

Despite the warning signs that were practically highway billboards, Martin was drawn to Nick. Nick reminded him of a wet, grumpy cat—not that he'd ever tell him that—a grumpy, wet cat who was not averse to kindness but also wasn't going to ask for it. Martin suspected about half of Nick's attitude was just how he was built and the other half stemmed from a life that had been unkind to Nick again and again.

Martin liked Nick's broody grumpiness, and he felt he was learning to speak "Nick." If he was bitching about something, it meant he cared about some aspect of it, and it pleased Martin to try and figure out what that aspect was.

An obvious example was the almost nightly rants about the tiny police department and how "they couldn't find their way around Cooper Springs with a hand-drawn map." The reality? Nick was upset that Lizzy Harlow's killer had, so far, gone unpunished and that Blair Cruz was still missing. No agency had even found a trace of her yet. It was as if she'd walked out of her friend's front door that Sunday and vanished into thin air.

Nick's attitude toward Martin had changed—softened—since their shopping trip before Christmas. Maybe it was that Martin believed him about the SUV. Maybe it was his relentless attempts to make Nick laugh by quoting lines from *Starsky and Hutch* anytime he could fit some in their conversation. He didn't know, but he was taking the win regardless.

After four-plus weeks with him around, Martin knew the younger man was intelligent, well-read, and had a rapier-sharp wit that kept Martin on his toes. The only person he had seen

Nick soft around was Liam Wright. Liam seemed to have some kind of special power that rendered Nick, if not helpless, at least less *bitey*.

As he stood there pondering life—and Nick—a lone firework whistled upward. Seconds later, it exploded into a shower of sparks that fell back toward the earth, creating a fountain of color. From the beach, Martin thought he heard cheering over the pounding of the surf.

Martin wondered where Nick was tonight. Was he down on the beach with the others, or had he decided to forego the celebration altogether? Martin thought Nick Waugh probably didn't care about New Year's Eve any more than he did Christmas.

Something irritatingly persistent inside of him wanted to get to know Nick even better—*intimately* better. Martin had been doing his best to squash these errant tendrils of *want,* but they returned daily, like the rodent in that whack-a-mole game.

He chuckled out loud at the image. "I am such an idiot."

Martin was curious about Nick's life, but he wasn't about to ask. The man did not give up personal information easily. He was gay. Martin was certain of that, in any case.

For Christ's sake, Martin still didn't know how or why he'd been shot. Although he did know that Nick was a vegetarian who loathed most vegetables. That he'd say no to an offer of tea or coffee, but if Martin handed it to him, he'd drink it. And that he still refused to give the kitten a name, even though it was obvious to Martin she wasn't going anywhere.

Stepping off the path, he surveyed his surroundings, looking for the best spot to sit. It was cold enough tonight that Martin's breath fogged in front of him. The last thing he wanted to do was sit too close to the edge; the fall would likely not be survivable.

Prickly or not, Nick did his part around the house. Made sure the dishes were clean and there was no clutter, even cooked meals once or twice, although those were experiences Martin would prefer not to repeat. And he'd worked just as hard—maybe harder—than the two guys Martin had brought in to work on the cabins.

"Nope, not going there," Martin said firmly.

Maybe if he said the words aloud, his subconscious would finally hear them and quit making him pause when he noticed the earthy smell of the soap Nick used. When Nick finally moved out, Martin was going to buy a case of it. Maybe two cases.

Even with so much moisture in the air, the odor of damp soil and pine needles was strong. Martin took a deep breath—this was his other new favorite scent. He glanced up to the night sky where a few faint stars were visible despite the misty clouds overhead. The wind was gusting, and it had a bite to it. But there was no rain; that much he would take any day.

"Happy New Year to me," Martin muttered as he peered around again, still searching for the perfect spot.

A voice floated from the inky darkness to Martin's left, asking, "You mind company?"

The voice was Nick's, of course, and not wholly unexpected. But Martin's heart still banged against his chest. He ignored it; this particular chest pain was nothing to worry about. Better ignored, in fact.

"Of course not," he replied. "But I only brought the one chair and I'm afraid in this case it's age before beauty."

Setting the camp chair down, Martin popped it open with one hand. Under his other arm he had a rolled-up fleece blanket and from his fingers dangled a large flask filled with a lot of whiskey, some hot water, a little bit of honey, and a couple of cinnamon sticks.

Nick stepped out of the shadows, a few stray beams of moonlight illuminating his angular features. He wasn't beautiful, not by any traditional measure. His face was all sharp corners, one eye was a slightly different shape than the other, and the left side of his mouth lifted slightly higher the rare times he smiled. But Martin, damn himself, was discovering Nick Waugh to be almost irresistible. Who could have predicted his kink was grumpy assholery?

"I don't need to sit down," Nick said.

Of course he didn't. Martin let a smile play across his lips. If Nick wanted to sit down, he'd sit down, when and where he wanted.

"Why aren't you at the beach with everyone else?" Martin asked, lowering himself into the chair.

"I could ask you the same question," Nick countered.

Martin shrugged. "Not really my thing. Mostly, I just wanted to see the stars and welcome in the new year." He held out the blanket he'd been planning to wrap around himself. "It's fleece with some kind of backing, probably meant for picnics."

Nick eyed Martin's offering before taking it. Unrolling it and flipping it open, he dropped the blanket to the ground next to Martin's chair and plopped down onto it, his long legs crossed at the ankles in front of him. All Martin had to do was reach out and he could touch him. He pushed his hand under his thigh to keep from doing just that.

"Any resolutions?" he asked.

Martin's resolution was: Don't do anything stupid. And especially don't try anything stupid with Nick.

Nick shook his head. "Nope. I always fuck them up anyway. What about you?"

Martin didn't answer; instead, he twisted the lid off the thermos and took a nice long sip. He didn't think he was the only one fighting an unexpected attraction. More than once, Martin had seen Nick watching him, a speculative, almost *hungry* expression on his face. This usually occurred when Martin wandered into the living room or kitchen without putting a shirt on first. He'd started "forgetting" to put a shirt on almost every morning since the first time he'd noticed Nick's reaction.

"Hot toddy. Want some?" Martin held out the flask.

Nick looked like he might not, but then, to Martin's surprise, he took the thermos and lifted it to his lips. Martin watched him, already feeling the whiskey invading his system, making him a little warmer and probably a lot reckless. Nick's Adam's apple moved as he swallowed, and Martin's cock twitched in response. A second later, Nick's eyebrows shot up as he coughed violently and glared back at Martin.

After wiping the back of his hand across his mouth, he managed to rasp, "Fucking Christ, is there any toddy in this, or is it straight whiskey?"

"My own special recipe. One part honey and water and the rest is pure Irish whiskey."

"Huh. You didn't say what your resolution is," Nick said, risking another drink from the thermos.

"Not to do anything stupid."

"So, buying a run-down resort—that, by the way, is merely cabins, so why the fuck is it called a resort?—was, or wasn't, last year's stupid?"

Nick handed the flask back to Martin.

"Buying this place is the best choice I've ever made. No, I'm talking about a different kind of stupid. And you're right, by the way," Martin continued, working to keep Nick from asking just what kind of stupid Martin had been referring to. "We need a new name. Maybe Cooper Springs Beachside Cabins."

Nick shook his head. "No flare. It needs to be more. Besides, they aren't really beachside. They're more beach-adjacent."

Another firework shot up over their heads and Martin took another drink. It was New Year's Eve, after all.

"That was my only idea. You've crushed my creative spirit."

Nick snickered, and Martin's cock twitched again. He tried to adjust his position to no avail.

"Hand me that whiskey again. Surely we can get the juices going with a little help."

Martin did as requested, leaving his hand in place so their fingertips touched during the exchange. Meeting Nick's gaze, Martin released the thermos, and now his dick was throbbing in time with his heartbeat. There was no way he could get up from his seat without his cock announcing its own resolution: A naked Nick Waugh, in his bed.

Raising the thermos to his lips again, Nick held his gaze. Martin couldn't have looked away if he'd wanted to. He really didn't want to.

"Detour."

"Excuse me." Martin shook his head. "What?"

"Detour. Detour back to 'not doing anything stupid.'" Nick set the whiskey down, making sure it wouldn't fall over.

A choking sound escaped Martin's throat, and Nick must have decided it meant to keep talking. It did not.

"What do you mean by stupid?" Nick asked softly.

Martin opened his mouth to answer, but no sound came out. Nick was rising to his knees and Martin didn't miss the bulge in the front of his jeans before Nick covered his own crotch and squeezed. "Would stupid be me having a fucking constant, massive hard-on around you? Would stupid be me sleeping on the fucking floor but wishing I was sharing your bed? And Fucking. Fucking. In. Your. Bed. I'm not making a resolution, but I do have a wish and you just heard it."

He wasn't aware of having made a choice. Of deciding to move. What Martin knew next was that he was finally tasting Nick Waugh's filthy fucking mouth. He tasted of whiskey and honey. Martin had one hand wrapped around the back of Nick's neck, holding him still so he could properly plunder his mouth and ravage him with his tongue.

So much for not doing anything stupid.

. . .

Abandoning the chair, the blanket, and the flask on the top of the bluff, they raced down the path. Martin didn't care if Bigfoot himself trespassed on the property to party, drink the rest of the whiskey, and make off with the chair and blanket.

They spilled in through the front door, and one of them shut it behind them. The lock clicked loudly in the silence. From her spot on the back of the couch, Kitten opened one yellow eye, watching them with kitten disgust.

Hands roamed across previously forbidden skin, tongues danced, and teeth clashed. Martin's cock ached with an urgency he hadn't felt in years. They stumbled into Martin's room, again shutting the door.

Spinning him around, Nick grabbed at the zipper of Martin's jeans and forced it down, then slipped his hand inside to grip his cock through his boxers. Nick moaned with satisfaction.

Martin had enough presence of mind to say, "Are you—"

Nick cut him off with, "If you leave me with blue balls after this, I will murder you in your sleep." Then he continued to peel Martin's jeans off his body. "Shit. Your boots. Sit," he ordered.

Martin sat on the edge of the bed with his legs spread as much as he could and his fully erect cock pointing at exactly what it wanted.

"Fucking hell, I am dying to taste that."

In a haze, Martin watched Nick lower himself to his knees, lean in, and drag his tongue along Martin's length. Without warning—or maybe licking him should have been warning—Nick's lips parted, and he proceeded to take Martin's cock into his mouth.

"Oh, my god," Martin whispered, leaning back on his hands so he could see better and do his valiant best not to thrust into his mouth. Nick's spit-wet lips wrapped around him were the most erotic thing he'd ever experienced. He wasn't going to last long, not with how much he'd been craving Nick over the last few weeks. Reality was far better than he'd allowed himself to imagine.

"Nick," he moaned, "please."

He knew Nick was smiling even with Martin's cock stuffed in his mouth. But he didn't pull off. Instead, he sucked harder, the tip of Martin's cock hitting the back of Nick's throat. He throbbed, his balls high and tight.

"Nick." Lifting up one hand, he used it to tug at Nick's head. "Not yet."

Relenting, Nick let Martin's cock slip from between his lips. Quickly, he reached down and untied Martin's stupid fucking boots, pulled them off his feet, and tossed them aside. Just as quickly, Nick was naked too.

Martin tugged his shirt over his head and got rid of the underwear. He felt a twinge of self-consciousness. He was in damn good shape, but he was twelve years older than Nick. Luckily, they hadn't turned on any of the lights.

"Condoms?" Nick asked.

Rolling to one side, Martin opened his bedside drawer. A reasonably new box of unopened condoms and a bottle of lube sat there. Nick snatched up the box, tore it open, and handed the condom to Martin. The lube he tossed onto the bed.

"I want you to fuck me."

Martin's cock, which wasn't sure what direction was up or down, pulsed, pushing out a dribble of precome.

As quickly as humanly possible, Martin ripped open the foil packet and rolled on the condom.

"Like riding a bike," he muttered.

Nick frowned. "What?"

"It's been a while."

"Ah, well then," Nick drawled, "lay back and let's get this party started."

Martin scooted all the way onto the bed and Nick followed after him, crawling on his hands and knees. His cock bounced against his stomach as he moved. Reaching out, Martin ran his fingers from the base to the tip.

"Don't distract me," Nick growled as he squeezed lube onto his fingers and reached back to make himself ready for Martin's cock.

It was all Martin could do to not grab Nick and demand he do this part. He wanted to push his fingers into that hot hole and make him ready. He should be the one to prep him and turn Nick into a puddle of goo begging for Martin's cock. Orders were not something Nick responded well to. But Martin was going to get his turn.

Nick groaned as he fingered himself and, after an eon, shuffled his knees up the sides of Martin's body so his ass hovered over Martin's erection.

"Ready?" Nick asked breathlessly.

Martin nodded, afraid that, if he spoke, the fever dream he was having would disappear and he would wake up with yet another hard-on.

Reaching down, Martin held his cock in place while Nick lowered his ass, slowly but surely, and impaled himself on Martin. Nick's eyes were shut, his lashes dark against his cheeks, and he moaned as he pushed downward. His cock flagged for a second but almost immediately hardened again as Martin popped past the resistant ring of muscle.

Nick groaned, "Oh, fuck me."

On Martin's part, the heat of Nick was almost his undoing. After the aborted blow job, he wasn't sure how much control he had left. Maybe none. A bead of sweat dripped down the side of his face as his throbbing cock made its way further inside Nick.

"Nick." Martin wasn't sure if he was begging or demanding.

Fully seated, Nick opened his eyes and smiled down at Martin. Then he began to move his body. Needing something— anything—to hold on to, Martin grabbed Nick's hips, helping him move while Martin moved inside him.

"You feel incredible," Martin gasped as Nick arched his back, and Martin forced his hips upward against gravity while Nick's body writhed and shuddered over him.

Releasing one hand from Nick's hip, Martin grasped the heavy cock bouncing in front of him. Precome leaked onto his chest, forming almost a puddle. Nick stared down at him through half-closed eyes.

"Yessss, please." Nick's voice was low, almost a whisper.

Wrapping his fingers around Nick's cock, Martin began to pump it. He could tell from the iron-hard feel of it in his hand that Nick was almost there. He pumped it only a few more times, adding a twist and using one long finger to caress Nick's tight balls.

Nick shouted, his hole clenching around Martin. He stiffened and threw his head back, his eyes shutting again, as come shot out his dick and soaked Martin's chest. The come and the wild abandon that was so unlike Nick Waugh sent Martin flying right over the edge after him.

NICK - NEW YEARS EVE TO NEW YEARS DAY

Fact: Washington State has a wide variety of rocks and a plethora of fossils, including crinoids, clams, trilobites, snails, corals, and at least one dinosaur. The state also has abundant petrified wood, which is the Washington State Gem, and has had over 40 Columbian Mammoth discoveries, which is the Washington State Fossil.

Martin Purdy was no fossil.

That's all Nick could think as he lay in the dark and stared up at the ceiling of Martin's bedroom. He would've left, but there didn't seem a point when leaving only meant walking fifteen feet and then trying to sleep on a couch not meant for that activity. A couch that was trying to kill him. And his ass ached; otherwise, he'd consider the floor.

So here Nick was, staring into the dark and wondering if maybe he had just done the stupidest thing in his life. Ever. More ridiculous than overreacting, emptying his bank account, and fleeing the country. Funny enough—he huffed a quiet laugh —that had also been associated with Martin Purdy.

Martin was asleep, his breathing soft and rhythmic. The man

fucked like a god *and* didn't snore. There was just so much for Nick to unpack, he didn't know where to begin. He'd had sex with the man he'd spent a good decade blaming for his life choices.

And he'd do it again if offered the chance.

After cleaning them both up, Martin had crawled back into bed and settled on the window side, leaving Nick *not trapped at all*, but wide fucking awake. He could get up and leave anytime he wanted and—well, sleep on a sleeping pad that made him feel like he'd aged eighty years by the time he woke up.

Martin hadn't even uttered the famous words, *We should talk.* He'd just rolled onto his side and fucking gone to sleep. Nick was mildly outraged. He didn't *want* to talk. He never *wanted* to talk, but… wasn't that what people usually said after an unexpected but fucking incredible bout of sex? He'd wanted Martin to say they should talk so he—Nick—could tell him to fuck off. But Martin had just fucking gone to sleep.

A low growl formed in Nick's throat. He bit his lips together to keep it from escaping.

Nick wished he could blame the sex on the whiskey, but neither of them had drunk that much. Certainly not enough to have an out-of-body experience involving Nick's ass and Martin's—very satisfying—dick. If Nick was going to be honest with himself, he had been hoping that Martin would skip the beach celebrations and stay home.

He'd had dinner with Liam, Forrest, Rufus, and Wanda at the pub. Turned down several invitations to come and join them and the rest of Cooper Springs at the beach. After much unnecessary chitchat about new year shit, he'd finally been on his way back to the resort when he'd seen Martin taking the trail up the bluff. His plan to sack out on the couch with the cat and the Harlan Coben novel he'd picked up at the thrift store had been immediately abandoned.

Tossed aside. Obliterated.

Without dwelling on what he thought he was doing, Nick had taken the path that started at the other end of the cabins and arrived at the top of the bluff at almost the same time as Martin. And damn, there was no denying the man was in good shape. Nick had been breathing harder than Martin after the climb.

And then. Well. Then something Nick had only imagined happening in his wildest fantasy had happened and had progressed at lightning speed. Zero to sixty in under three seconds. To be honest, he'd followed Martin with the express intention of engineering exactly what had happened although he hadn't expected it to be a fucking tidal wave that he had been unable—and hadn't wanted—to escape.

Flopping over onto his side, Nick faced Martin's back and his wide, strong shoulders. He was briefly tempted to scoot a little closer.

Probably he should ease out from under the covers and head to the sleeping pad. He would just lie here a little longer.

When Nick opened his eyes again, it was daylight and Kitten was curled up next to him. He was stretched out on his stomach —clearly, his body was happy not to be on the floor. Hissing and clinking sounds that Nick was now familiar with came from the kitchen. Martin was up and already puttering around.

He was debating getting up and trying to find his clothes when Martin padded back into the bedroom carrying a steaming mug.

"Ready for coffee?" Martin asked.

He sat up and dislodged Kitten in the process. She hopped off the bed and departed, her tail stiff with indignation. Nick nodded, managing a hoarse, "Thanks." Martin set the cup on the bedside table. The drawer hadn't been shut all the way, so the bottle of lube lay in plain sight.

Martin caught the direction of Nick's gaze and a slight smile played across his lips, but all he said was, "Breakfast will be ready in about ten minutes, if you want to shower or anything."

"Breakfast?"

"New Year's breakfast. Gotta start the year off right."

Nick nodded, not really knowing what to think about a New Year's breakfast. Or Martin continuing to accept his presence without question. The longer he stayed with Martin, the softer Nick got. He needed to remind himself that the world was not kind and especially not kind to the likes of Nick Waugh.

"Blueberry waffles, maple syrup, and, if you're lucky, I'll save you a vegetarian sausage patty."

Nick's stomach growled, and Martin shot him a grin. Damn, that was a dangerous smile. Apparently, Nick was going to remind himself about the ways of the world at a later time.

"So, what's the plan today?" Nick asked around a bite of the best waffle he'd ever had. He'd managed a shower and found his jeans tossed over the arm of the couch.

Martin glanced out the window, and so did Nick. The sun was shining and there were only a few clouds overhead. It would be cold, but it didn't seem like there was a chance of rain.

"Since the weather is holding and the rest of the panels finally arrived, I really want to get the roof to Cabin Five finished. But the guys aren't coming today, so we should just take the day off."

"Seems a shame to waste a decent day's weather." Nick wasn't sure how he felt about *his* cabin coming closer to being livable. It gave him a twitchy feeling in his stomach.

Martin waggled his head in semi-disagreement. "I suppose. But the weather is supposed to hold all week, so executive decision. Day off, it is. I didn't change my life just to work day in and day out. So," he finished, pointing his fork at Nick, "what is there to do?"

There wasn't much to do on New Year's Day in or around Cooper Springs. Except—

"Not the fucking Polar Bear Swim that Forrest was going on about. I like my balls the way they are. I don't want them permanently retreating into my body."

"Noted. No Polar Bear Swim. Maybe next year."

"I'd have to lose a major bet for that to happen. No way."

Martin just smiled and popped another bite of waffle into his mouth.

Looking out the window, Nick's gaze snagged on the evergreen trees near the bottom of the slope that made up the backside of the bluff. Martin walked up there almost every day.

"One of us should get the stuff we left up the hill last night," Nick said.

"Already taken care of," Martin replied, nodding in the direction of the sink.

Nick saw the thermos propped in the dish drainer. Martin had already been up and back. Just how long had Martin been awake? And Nick had been so deeply asleep he hadn't heard him moving around. When was the last time he'd slept that hard?

"There's Crook's Trail," Nick offered. Crook's Trail was the gem trail in the region. During the summer months, it drew ardent hikers and backpackers to Cooper Springs.

Martin looked interested. "Is it doable this time of year? With all the rain we've had?"

"Yeah, it's pretty well maintained. There's a great viewpoint about three miles in, where the forest sort of parts and you can see all the way to the ocean and down the coast towards Ocean Shores and Westport too. It's pretty cool. I wouldn't go all the way to the lakes alone if I were you, but yeah, it's doable."

"It's a good thing I'm not going alone, then. You're going

with me," Martin informed him.

Nick blinked. "What? No."

"Yes. You wouldn't want the old man disappearing in the wilds, would you? I need a hiking buddy and I gave you the day off. Therefore, you're coming with me. And don't try telling me you don't have any hiking gear because I've seen your stuff, and that's about all you have."

Damn.

"Finish your breakfast and get ready," Martin said authoritatively. "I'll make some grub for us to take along."

Nick blinked again, unsure exactly how he'd ended up being bossed around by Martin Purdy. He opened his mouth to tell Martin to fuck off, or something equally astounding, but instead what came out was, "Not peanut butter. I hate peanut butter."

"Noted. Now go get properly dressed."

Truly, they couldn't have ordered a better day for a winter hike in the Olympics. There were only a few clouds drifting across the sky and the temperature had almost reached the fifties before noon. Not too hot and not too cold. Even better, there didn't seem to be anyone else with the idea that New Year's Day was a great day to hike.

Since he'd been back in Cooper Springs, Nick hadn't visited the forest more than once or twice, and he hadn't hiked Crook's Trail at all. He'd always loved this particular trail but—if he was going to be honest with himself—he'd been hesitant to trek into the woods after his injury. He didn't completely trust his leg, and he hated the feeling that something, someone, might appear out of nowhere and attack him, which was what had happened in Sri Lanka.

Crook's Trail was not a vibrant city market. There would be no random attack, he reassured himself. There were no stalls festooned with colorful fabrics and displays of fruits, vegetables, and spices. And there were also no crowds of people milling about and pushing past each other, intent on doing their daily errands, looking for what they needed to make dinner that night.

Still, Nick felt… safer with Martin plodding along beside him, not talking too much but occasionally pointing at various rocks and boulders along the way and easily naming what they were made of. The one that looked like a rabbit was basalt.

"This is beautiful, Nick. Great idea," Martin said when they were about a mile along the trail. They had been slowly gaining elevation, but Nick thought he remembered that soon the path turned into a long stretch of what seemed like vertical switchbacks.

"I feel like this was your idea. I'm not really sure how I ended up here," Nick groused.

"Admit it, you love it."

"It's alright," Nick conceded just as a large crow swooped directly over their heads. He stared after it, watching as the bird abruptly changed direction and headed toward an open area where the trees had grown in a sort of circle. "That's a raven, isn't it?"

Nick stopped walking. They weren't in a hurry after all.

"Think so," Martin said, also watching the bird.

"I read somewhere that ravens live all over Washington, just not in any of the big cities."

"That makes sense," Martin agreed. "They'd have a hard time competing with all the crows for food and nest space, in Seattle anyway. At my old house, I used to watch the crows come home at dusk. Always an intense experience, witnessing hundreds of crows flying together, intent on returning to their rookery. A big, long line of them all heading in the same direction—very Edgar Allan Poe-ish."

Martin started walking again. Nick stared after him for ten seconds before jogging to catch up. Martin Purdy was full of surprises. Who would have expected a geology professor to have a poetic side?

They continued walking in silence for another mile or so, the only sounds coming from the forest itself—the drip of moisture off leaves and pine needles, the huff of a breeze that disturbed the canopy above them, sending random showers down on their heads.

"Why did you move to Cooper Springs?" This was something Nick had been curious about since Martin first arrived. Since the minute Nick had recognized him standing beside Xavier in the parking lot.

Martin glanced over at him before answering Nick's question. "I had a heart attack."

"A heart attack?" Nick sputtered, almost tripping on a tree root. Martin grabbed his shoulder to keep him from face-planting. That was not the answer Nick had expected. He'd thought it would be something like Martin wanting to commune with nature. Not that he'd nearly died.

"Yep." Martin seemed to pick up the pace.

"A heart attack?" he repeated. "I mean—how? You're like the fittest person I know."

"Well, I wasn't before, but I work hard at keeping fit now. I just let myself get entrenched in academic life and it took its toll. This," he said as he waved a hand that encompassed the whole forest and everything inhabiting it, "is so much better."

His fitness was evident by the way Martin relentlessly kept moving, taking the switchbacks with ease. Nick was beginning to suspect that was Martin's approach to life in general. Nick's thigh muscles were burning, and he was trying not to pant. Lucky for him, he had a great view of Martin's ass.

"How did you get shot?" Martin asked out of the blue. The question seemed intrusive, even if Nick had just been prying into Martin's private life. He figured Martin had heard about it from someone in town. Magnus was Nick's bet, but it could have been Forrest. And there'd been a few times in the past month that Martin could have spotted the knotty scar on his upper thigh.

"A bad case of wrong place, right time," Nick replied. Fuck, he might as well tell Martin the whole story. "I was doing some freelance work for a travel site and ended up in the middle of a gunfight in Colombo."

"I didn't realize Sri Lanka was that dangerous."

"Neither did I," Nick agreed. "And apparently, it normally isn't. *I* was just lucky enough to get caught in the middle of a business disagreement."

"And then you came back here?"

They turned up another switchback, passing by an enormous and ancient nurse tree. Three younger trees had grown from it and were already fifty feet tall. Tiny delicate ferns dotted the nurse trunk where jade-green moss had left space for them to take hold.

Nick considered what else he would share with Martin about the shooting. "I was held hostage for a day—at least that's what they tell me. I don't actually remember much after, not until I woke up in the hospital. Even then, it took me a while to get stateside."

Mostly, he remembered when he dreamed. The pain, the fear, his heart beating too loudly. The woman who owned the fruit stall leaning over him, trying to stop the flow of blood.

"What about your family, your parents? Did they help you get home?"

Nick was debating how much he wanted to share about his lack of family when he spotted something off the trail that made him pause. Martin, not realizing Nick had stopped, kept on walking.

A tree had fallen about sixty feet off the side of the trail. Recently too. It looked like a hemlock to Nick, but he'd have to get closer before he knew for sure. The now exposed dirt-encased root ball was easily taller than Nick or Martin. The tree had been an old one. The last big storm must have been too much for it. There was just *something* about the roots that seemed weird to his eye. Something that didn't make sense.

With the voices of both Critter and Mags bitching in his head about hikers who went "stomping" off trails and inadvertently crushed rare native plants like trillium and the stream orchid, Nick gingerly moved toward the tree, watching every step.

"Nick," Martin called out, finally realizing he wasn't behind him any longer. "What are you doing?" He jogged back toward the spot where Nick had left the path.

"Just a sec, I need to check something."

Carefully watching his every step, Nick approached the fallen tree. He felt a bit silly—the tree, after all, wasn't going to attack him. *Trees That Attack*, he snickered. That would be a great title for a horror novel.

The closer he got, the more certain he became that he had actually seen something. Something very wrong.

"Fuck," he muttered, staring up at the massive root ball full of rocks, chucks of earth and—"Fuck, fuck, fuck."

"What is—shit, is that a skull?"

Martin had followed him, standing close enough now that their shoulders touched.

"I'm no forensic scientist, although I have watched a lot of *NCIS*, but I have the feeling that is, indeed, a human skull."

As much as it pained Nick to agree with Martin—that one of them should remain behind *just in case*, the other returning to town to alert the authorities—Nick stayed back at the site while Martin headed back. His thigh ached, although he didn't admit that to Martin. Nick watched him jog down the hill, and when he disappeared around a far bend in the path, Nick picked his way back to the tree.

"How long have you been here?" Nick asked the skull.

There was no answer, of course.

The skull appeared to be embedded on the outermost edge of the root ball—that was what had caught Nick's attention, the wrongness of it. Peering closer, he tried to see if there were more parts, more bones. He didn't see anything obvious, but they could have been carried off by scavengers or buried more deeply, where they were difficult to find.

As he'd told Martin, he wasn't an expert. But Nick had seen his fair share of calcified human remains. Early in his career, he'd been hired by a group of forensic anthropologists to photograph their findings and help them identify victims buried in mass graves in southern Mexico. So he had, in fact, seen many human remains.

Regardless of what he'd said to Martin, Nick knew the skull had once belonged to a human.

"Who are you?" he wondered out loud.

A raven, maybe even the same one he and Martin had seen earlier, fluttered down from above and landed on top of the exposed roots.

"Do you know, raven?"

The bird cocked its head as if it was trying to think of an answer.

Nick suspected the remains had been there for some time. A year, possibly many years. As far as he knew, there were no unaccounted-for hikers, not in the last decade or so. There was the girl who disappeared last summer, and Blair Cruz, but this skull couldn't be either of theirs. He didn't think so anyway. The cops hadn't yet identified the bones found last month and those had been further up anyway, closer to the lakes. Nick doubted they were related.

"Who the *fuck* is responsible for this?"

The raven cawed, the sound eerily loud and jarring. Then, apparently deciding Nick was boring, the ebony-black bird flew off again and disappeared into the forest.

MARTIN

Fact: Rivers within the Olympics mountain range form a radial drainage pattern, meaning they flow away from the center of the ancient volcanic uplift. These rivers carry colossal amounts of water from the top of the Olympic Mountains, where it rains an average of 140 to 200 inches a year (more than any other place in the continental United States), down to the Pacific Ocean.

Martin sighed, thankful to finally be left on his own. Conversation flowed around him, and for the time being, at any rate, he was not the center of attention. Nick, he noticed, had disappeared. Or, more likely, the residents of Cooper Springs knew better than to trap Nick Waugh and pummel him with questions.

Finding human remains was not what Martin had envisioned for the first day of the new year.

It had taken him less than an hour to jog back down the trail. Thirty minutes to rally the troops. And another hour to lead them back up to Nick. He supposed it hadn't actually been him doing the rallying, but it seemed like it had taken forever for the police to get their act together.

Yes, it was only a skull, *as far as they knew*. The person whose skull it had been was long gone. But Martin didn't like the idea of Nick being up there all alone.

Chief Dear had been off duty when Martin arrived, panting and sweaty, at the police station. The deputy at the front desk reluctantly called to notify their boss, wincing when Dear answered with a gruff, *"For god's sake, what?"* that Martin had heard from across the lobby.

Martin felt bad that Dear's day off had been cut short. He doubted the chief got many of those. He'd wanted to leave and get back to Nick, but another deputy, Lani Cooper, had informed him he needed to wait for the chief and suggested that he probably didn't need to hike back up.

Yeah, no.

It had been almost two in the afternoon by the time the team of four—five, if he counted himself—started back up the trail. Martin led the way, even though he knew perfectly well the Forest Service officers would be able to find Nick and the remains on their own.

"Whoever it is, is way past saving," Dear said between attempts to drag air into his lungs, "unless there's something you're not telling us."

Martin had ignored Dear and kept up the pace. Maybe the chief needed to consider a new fitness regime.

"You ever do any of the mud runs?" Critter asked him with what sounded like appreciation. He had no problem keeping up with Martin and neither did the other officer, Mags.

"Nope. But maybe I will now. I've never had the time before." And he wasn't going to tell them the only reason he was in good shape now was because he'd had a "cardiac event."

They passed the boulder that looked like a rabbit. Martin calculated they were about a mile out.

"How much further?" Dear asked.

"Chief, you're worse than a five-year-old. I'm sure we'll know when we get there." That was Deputy Cooper. Martin liked her better and better with every step they took.

Finally, they rounded the last bend before the newly fallen tree.

"Took you long enough," Nick called from where he waited, his hands jammed into the pockets of his jacket. "I'm freezing."

"You didn't have to stay back," Mags pointed out. "Whoever it is won't be going anywhere."

Nick scowled and shrugged, not looking at anyone in particular. "It didn't seem right to just leave them. Not now that they're exposed to the elements."

They'd brought a tarp, rope, a camera, and whatnot along with them. But there wasn't much daylight left, so they were going to need to hurry. And, in Martin's opinion, they needed to do something to secure the site.

"Where are we looking?" Dear asked.

Gesturing for Dear to follow him, Nick stepped off the trail. Martin had decided to stay back. He'd already seen it; they didn't need him. The rest of the group had followed Nick and the chief.

"How's Nick doing?"

Martin looked up from the coffee Magnus had set in front of him a half hour ago. It was cold now because every time he started to take a sip, someone wanted to ask him questions. Screw the coffee, he was going to need a beer.

The question came from a man about Nick's age. Martin thought he recognized him as Nick's friend, Liam, but they'd never been introduced.

"Fine, I think," he said. "Although he seems to have escaped somewhere. I don't think we've officially met. Martin Purdy."

"Liam Wright," Liam said, shaking Martin's hand. "Yeah, Nick's not big on crowds."

"This certainly seems to have brought the entire town out."

Liam grimaced. "Ghouls, many of them. No offense or anything. I love my town, but I'd bet a dollar that a few showed up hoping to get a look at what you found."

"Huh," Martin grunted, feeling like he needed a beer more than ever.

After securing the scene as best they could, they'd all hiked back into town. Chief Dear had immediately contacted the mayor, Roslyn Moore, and that had led to this impromptu Town Hall.

They'd taken over the Steam Donkey. It was the only place in town with space to hold a crowd and, apparently, it was where the adult population of Cooper Springs headed when there was any kind of big news anyway. Martin figured Pizza Mart served the same purpose for teens.

When they arrived, Martin had immediately been bombarded by people he didn't know, asking him questions he couldn't answer. Finally, Magnus took pity and rescued him, giving him a cup of coffee and leading him to an empty table with a *Reserved* sign sitting on it. That was when he'd realized Nick had disappeared.

"Do you mind if I share your table?" Liam asked. "I want to hear what Roslyn has to say."

"Oh, is the mayor going to speak?" Martin asked.

Liam nodded toward the dance-slash-stage area. "I think both she and Dear are going to give statements."

The chatter in the pub quieted and sure enough, Chief Dear had taken the stage. Standing next to him was a diminutive, dark-haired woman who looked to be in her midsixties. She was much shorter than the chief and seemed to be trying to make up for it with six-inch heels. All Martin could think was, why would anyone living in Cooper Springs wear high heels?

Incredibly, everyone stopped talking. The only sounds were the hum of the coolers behind the bar and the hiss of something in the kitchen area.

"Good afternoon, or evening, as the case is," the mayor began. "As you all seem to already be aware, a second set of remains was discovered this afternoon on Crook's Trail."

The murmuring began to increase, but Mayor Moore held up her hand, hushing them. "Before you ask, no, we don't know who it is. We are doing everything in our power to identify this person." She looked around the room, her dark eyes hesitating on Martin—leastways, it felt like they did—before moving on. "We will use every resource available to us."

Someone grumbled, "Right. A couple of dropout deputies with a mail-order forensics kit they ordered off a sketchy online company."

The chief's eyes narrowed. He may not have been in the best hiking shape, but the man had good hearing. His steely gaze swept the room until it landed on the culprit. A flash of irritation was followed by his steel-gray eyebrows rising slightly. Leaning a bit to the side, Martin peered over at the man who'd spoken. It was no one he knew, but he had the sneaking suspicion that Dear might.

From where Martin was sitting, he could see the guy was built. He had massive shoulders, wider than Martin's anyway. He must've felt Martin looking at him because, twisting around in his chair, he practically skewered Martin with an ice-blue glare. Martin wasn't the kind of person who usually noticed that kind of stuff—except for Nick's, for some reason—but the guy's eyes were lasers that pierced right through a person.

The front door opened and Xavier Stone and Vincent Barone stepped inside, breaking the weird standoff. Spotting Martin, Xavier smiled and headed his way.

"Can we share your table?" Xavier asked.

Martin gestured at the empty seats. "Be my guest."

Xavier took the seat next to Martin while Vincent sat by Liam and turned his chair so he'd be able to see the stage and the two people occupying it.

"I feel like I was late to homeroom," Xavier whispered.

The mayor cleared her throat and the crowd quieted. Her impossibly crimson lips turned down and her eyebrows drew together. She did not appear impressed, but maybe that was how she always looked. Martin hadn't met her in person yet.

"Thank you all for coming out. I'm giving the stage to Chief Dear for now. He's going to fill us all in on the situation."

Dear stepped forward. "Thank you, Mayor Moore." He gazed out over the crowd, his glance pausing on the man sitting kitty-corner from Martin. Seeming to realize he was taking too long, Dear shook his head and began. He didn't share any information Martin didn't already know, especially seeing as it had only been a few hours since they'd all traipsed back down Crook's Trail.

There had been a brief discussion over whether someone should stay behind and protect the scene since Crook's Trail was public. In the end, they'd decided to declare the trail closed and string tape across the path to keep people from heading up to see what they could see. From the expression on Critter's face, Martin suspected he would be snoozing in his car at the trail entrance in an attempt to keep looky-loos away.

Dear stopped talking and stepped back. The mayor stepped forward again.

"I realize," she declared, directing her glare at the man who'd made the mail-order forensics comment, "that Cooper Springs doesn't have all the resources it needs to solve this crime, and we are still waiting to learn more about the remains discovered back in October. Soon, we'll have a little more help. West Coast Forensics has offered us their assistance."

"Friends in high places," Laser-Eye Guy muttered. "Maybe they'll actually solve this."

"My son, actually," Moore responded. "But yes." She looked

around, taking in everyone in the pub. "There are more resources on the way. We *will* get to the bottom of this."

"It would be nice if it was before anyone else goes missing." If the guy was trying to mutter, his effort failed. Martin suspected he didn't give a crap who heard him.

Chief Dear's dark scowl clearly expressed his belief that if murder weren't illegal, he'd have a go at the asshole. And it was a miracle the mystery man didn't burst into flames when Mayor Moore shot him the evil eye.

"We are doing everything we can," Dear said into the following silence. He stepped to the front of the stage again. "Please, respect my deputies as we work the scene. If anyone thinks they might have information about this person, or the remains discovered in the fall, please contact the police department."

The stranger's massive shoulders moved up and back down in a careless shrug. He was trying to antagonize the chief—and it was working.

"I'm warning you all now, if one more person calls the station claiming it was Bigfoot or"—he grimaced—"the Sasquatch, I swear by all that is holy, I will send a deputy to your home and have you charged with impeding an investigation."

"Tough call, Chief." Shoulder Man again.

"What's that guy's problem?" Liam wanted to know.

Chief Dear's nostrils flared and even from where he was sitting, Martin saw the muscle along his jaw clench. His lips parted and he started forward. Luckily, the mayor put a restraining hand on the chief's arm, possibly saving the stranger's life. Or Dear's.

"Anybody know who he is?" Martin asked quietly. He had no intention of getting into it with the self-appointed know-it-all.

"Not sure, but I've seen him around town," responded Liam.

"That's Dante Brown," Vincent informed them. "His niece,

Daniella, was in one of my classes this past fall. They just moved to town. I think they live somewhere near the mansion."

"Dante Brown, huh?" Xavier repeated, squinting at the guy. "He's built like a brick shit house." Xavier reached over and pinched Vincent's thick biceps. "You are too, baby. The only brick house I care about."

Vincent rolled his eyes, but Martin could tell he was secretly pleased. "They moved to town after the school year started," Vincent added. "I'm trying to get Romy to befriend Daniella. But you know how teenagers are."

Romy was Vincent's teenaged daughter. Martin had seen her walking Wanda's and Xavier's dogs in the afternoons. And he did have an idea how teenagers were, certainly college-aged ones. Martin missed absolutely nothing about standing in front of a lecture hall full of hormone-addled students.

"It looks like this is over, so I'm going to escape while everyone is trying to talk to Dear," Martin told the rest of the table as he stood up from his seat.

Liam nodded, pushing his hair behind his ear. "Get out of here. Track Nick down and make sure he's doing okay."

Nick was back at the cabin. Martin had half-expected him to have disappeared somewhere.

"There you are," he said as he shut the door behind himself. "Can't believe you deserted me with the vultures. Now I know what it feels like to be attacked by a school of piranha."

Nick looked up from where he was sitting on the couch. For the first time Martin was aware of, Nick was doing something on his laptop. An empty mug sat on the coffee table. Kitten was perched on the windowsill.

Smiling at Nick—and at the kitten—Martin realized he *liked* finding him there. And it wasn't because he was lonely. It was because he liked Nick. A lot. Not sure if he should be worried about this revelation, he shoved the thought aside for the moment and focused instead on the fact that they'd never had lunch and now it was dinnertime. After the longer-than-expected hike, he was famished.

"I couldn't deal with everyone," Nick said in a way that hinted at apology. "There's a reason I'm a photographer. I like being on the anonymous side of the camera."

Huh. That was possibly the most revealing piece of information Nick had ever shared with Martin.

"Well, I'm used to rocks," Martin said. "They don't talk back. You want a beer?"

Nick eyed his mug. "Sure, yeah. A beer sounds good."

Heading toward the kitchen for a beer he could drink in peace—and to stare at the contents of the fridge—Martin paused. He'd worried about Nick while he'd gone for help. Nothing specific, just a vague sense of unease at leaving him alone with a human skull.

Which was ridiculous. This wasn't *Deliverance,* and even if Simon joked about it, chainsaw-wielding serial killers were a figment of Hollywood's imagination.

"You doing okay after all that? Do you need to talk about anything?" he asked.

The expression on Nick's face was priceless. He looked like he'd sucked on a lemon and stepped barefoot in dog crap at the same time.

"No, I fucking don't want to talk about anything."

"Alright then, we'll just keep on going on. Beer, or something stronger?"

Nick perked up. "Whiskey?"

"Ah, yes." Martin stepped into the kitchen, opening the cabinet where he'd stashed his whiskey collection. "Straight or what?"

There was a rustling, creaking sound and then Martin could feel Nick standing behind him.

"Or what works," Nick replied.

"Old-fashioned, it is. Go sit down, you're in my way."

Nick chose to sit at the kitchen table instead of retreating back to the couch. Martin suspected he did want to talk but would only admit it on threat of death, or torture, or something else ridiculous.

Martin busied himself with locating the ingredients he needed. Lemon, bitters, simple syrup. And thinking about dinner. The sandwiches he'd thrown together hours ago no longer appealed and were likely smashed after being in his back-pack all day.

"How'd you escape the interrogation, anyway?" Martin asked.

"Just left, and nobody stopped me. You were being mobbed by the curiosity crowd. I saw my advantage and took it."

"Ah." Martin set about muddling the simple syrup with the bitters, then added a healthy couple of fingers of whiskey. He topped it off with a slender twist of lemon zest. "Here ya go." Carefully placing Nick's drink in front of him, Martin sat down at the end of the tiny table.

"Did you learn anything?" Nick finally asked.

Martin resisted smiling; Nick was nothing if not curious.

"Nope. Not really."

"Huh."

"I feel kind of bad for Chief Dear."

"Why? Catching criminals is his literal job."

Martin waggled his head. "Yes, but this is a small town. How big is the force, like ten people?"

"Eleven. If you count Carol Page, who sometimes answers the phones."

"Okay, so eleven. And no money. There was this one guy there, riding him hard."

"Oh?" Nick's eyebrows lifted.

"The thing is, what he pointed out isn't wrong—although,

hopefully, CSPD doesn't order their forensic kits off the internet."

"He said that? In public? Seriously, who was this guy?"

"Liam didn't know him. Vincent Barone said he was new to town. He and his niece live somewhere by the mansion. Uh, Dante Brown. Vincent had his niece in his class or something."

"By the mansion?" Nick had lifted his glass but set it back down on the table.

"I think that's what he said. Why?"

A shifty, possibly embarrassed, expression flitted across Nick's face.

"Nothing."

Setting his own glass back down, Martin watched Nick and waited. Nick looked out the window, but since dark had fallen, there wasn't much to see now.

Martin had been studying the Book of Nick for weeks now. The first chapter was Be Patient. He wanted to believe that Nick was learning to trust him—and, after last night, that hope had begun to blossom.

NICK

Sir Martin Frobisher, an English privateer and explorer, brought back 1,350 tons of what he thought was gold ore to Queen Elizabeth in 1578. Unfortunately for Sir Frobisher, the ore actually was mostly iron pyrite—fool's gold.

Dammit.

Nick pretended he was looking at the cabins, even though all he could see were the outside walls of the one closest to Martin's. In reality, he was remembering the black SUV and how it had disappeared down the street the mansion was built on. Possibly, he *had* overreacted. Maybe this jackass, Dante Brown, owned the car and Liam and everyone else were right— he was seeing things that just weren't there.

In the weeks since the spotting the men-in-black Toyota Sequoia in Aberdeen, Nick had mostly put the SUV out of his mind—as well as the death of Lizzy Harlow. Hot sex did that to a man. And maybe the fact that when he'd told Martin about his suspicion that it was up to no good, Martin hadn't questioned him. He'd taken Nick's misgivings at face value. Just like that, without having to explain anything. And even though it had been a lost cause by that point, Martin had tried to follow the vehicle.

Martin, who was patiently waiting for him to say something. Martin, who was quickly becoming important. He'd been slipping under Nick's defenses even before last night.

"Nothing, really," Nick muttered. Hoping Martin would leave it at that. And he probably would, which is why Nick wanted to tell him.

He shifted his gaze back to Martin, who was sipping at his old-fashioned, acting like Nick's weirdness was totally normal. Not judging or demanding. Just... waiting.

"There's—" Nick started.

At the same time, Martin said, "I forgot to mention. Mayor Moore has managed to arrange for a private forensics company to assist with the investigation."

Nick's eyebrows shot up and he leaned forward. If Martin hadn't had his full attention already, he sure had it now. "Yeah? Really? Who is it?"

"West Coast Forensics. Have you heard of them?"

"No. But that's what the internet is for."

Martin rose to his feet. "You look them up while I figure out dinner. I'm starving after today." He stretched, his form-fitting t-shirt somehow barely managing not to burst at the seams. Nick had recurring dreams about that shirt and all the ways he could help Martin peel it off his body.

"Stir-fry okay?"

Nick nodded. Frankly, everything Martin cooked was worth putting in his mouth. Same with Martin's cock. His face felt suddenly hot. He'd mostly avoided thinking about what had happened last night, but now his brain decided he needed a Technicolor replay. In slow motion.

"Yes," he choked out, "stir-fry sounds fine. I'll just—" he started to rise, then realized halfway up that his dick had decided to join in on the fun and games too. It was the damn shirt. It outlined everything incredible about Martin's body. Martin's t-shirts should always be just a tad too small.

"You okay there?"

"Yep. Just gonna grab my laptop"—he pointed to the living room as if Martin didn't already know where he was headed—"and check out this West Coast Forensics outfit."

Martin chose that moment to open the fridge door, bending down to see what was in the vegetable chiller. *That ass.* Nick's cock twitched. Giving up on himself, Nick huffed out to the living room, erection and all, and snatched his laptop up from where he'd left it.

Back at the kitchen table, Nick opened his computer and started a search.

"Mmm, let's see here. West Coast Forensics... Ah, here it is. The company was founded by a guy named Kimball Frye, who was an arson investigator with the ATF before that. They're based out of Oakland, and—Piedras Island? What the hell. Anyway, now there's a partner, Leo Zelinsky. His specialty is cold cases, used to be a cop in Seattle. They have several homicide investigators." He kept reading, skimming through the information provided. "They also offer services and education to small police forces. Chief Dear should look into that."

He clicked into the list of employees, wondering who would be coming to Cooper Springs.

"Awards, commendations, blah blah blah. Ohhh, who do we have here?" Nick clicked into the bio information listed next to a crap photograph of one Ethan Moore.

"What?" Martin asked over his shoulder as he finished chopping some onions and moved on to a couple of cloves of garlic.

"I found the connection. Ethan Moore. Unless I'm totally off-base—and I don't think I am—he's the mayor's son. It says here he's a forensic anthropologist. Cool, cool. He might actually be useful."

"A forensic anthropologist. That's good, isn't it?"

"*I* think so. I've worked with a few. They're generally smart and motivated to find the truth."

The FAs Nick had worked with in Mexico had been driven, intelligent people intent on doing what they could to bring closure—and justice—to victims' loved ones.

"Did you know this guy?" Martin asked. "Ethan Moore?"

Nick shook his head before realizing that Martin was paying attention to the knife in his hand and not Nick.

"Nope. He has to be at least five or six years older than me."

"Ah, yes, practically ancient, on his deathbed," Martin interjected, his tone amused.

"Fuck off." He raised his middle finger for emphasis. "Moore and I wouldn't have been in school at the same time. And besides, my parents didn't move here until I was nine, so, ya know, I was the new kid."

Martin quit chopping, turned around, and leaned back against the counter to face Nick. "Why did your family move here?"

Nick froze. It was a perfectly innocent question, but fuck if he hadn't managed to avoid all mention of his parents until this very second. What innocuous fact could he drag out from his well of memories?

"My dad was an engineer. He worked for some of the last logging companies in the area."

"Was? I mean, not to pry or anything."

"They live in Florida now. Or they did, last time I knew anything about them."

Martin's salt-and-pepper eyebrows drew together. "Did they kick you out?"

This was Nick's chance, the point where he could lie and say yes. He could skip past the part about actually being in Martin's geology lecture. But his lips refused to form those words.

"Ah, no. The gay thing is the least of my failings, not that I ever knew what most of them were. We haven't talked since I failed out of the UW."

Martin cocked his head and stared intently at Nick, his eyes narrowing as comprehension dawned.

"You were in my class, weren't you? *I knew it.*"

Martin crossed his arms over his chest and he chewed at his bottom lip, thinking, trying to place Nick. For his part, Nick felt like a spotlight had been turned on and pointed directly at him. The silence stretched thin as Martin kept staring at him, and Nick's brain refused to come up with anything but the truth.

Finally, Nick settled with nodding.

"Am I right in assuming my lecture had something to do with your failing out?" Martin asked. "I thought you seemed familiar. But honestly, the classes were so large, it was impossible to know all my students. That must have been ten or twelve years ago, right?"

"Twelve and change," Nick grumbled, not wanting his anger toward Martin to soften further. He needed something to keep his other feelings about him at bay. It was bad enough the sex had been literally fucking incredible. He needed to remember that living in Martin's cabin wasn't permanent. Nick wasn't permanent. There was no way an intelligent man like Martin Purdy would want to keep someone like Nick around.

Not that Nick wanted that, either. Nope.

"If it means anything, I'm sorry that happened to you," Martin offered, surprising Nick. "The academic machine can be a bastard. A faceless machine doesn't recognize individuals and certainly doesn't make a great enough effort to help those who need it. But your parents"—Martin scowled, taking Nick by surprise—"just... fucked off?"

"I really don't want to talk about this."

"Not ever or not right now?"

"Not ever, but I'll settle for not right now."

"Sure, I can respect that. But I am sorry." The scowl

morphed into a positively evil smile. "But not about what happened last night. Just to make that crystal clear."

Turning back around, Martin pulled out a skillet and turned on the stove, humming as he did so. Nick stared at his back for a long minute before returning to the West Coast Forensics website.

"Nick, get in bed with me," Martin ordered. "Or make yourself comfortable on the floor if you insist on that nonsense. But quit standing out there, you're making the floorboards creak."

Nick grimaced; he didn't *want* to sleep on the floor. It was where he *should* sleep. He stared at Kitten tucked into the corner of the couch. She stared back at him with an expression that said, *Don't look at me, I'm perfectly comfortable.*

Dinner had been great, as usual. Martin was a good cook. Afterwards, Nick cleaned up the mess and straightened the kitchen while Martin sat at the table, checked emails, and made triple sure that Dane and Zeke, the guys he'd hired to help them out with the cabins, were still coming the next day.

Then Martin had announced he was taking a shower and going to bed.

"It's been a damn long day. I'm going to bed," he'd said as he'd left the kitchen. A minute later, the shower had come on. Almost immediately, Nick had been assailed with visions of a naked Martin standing under the spray, soaping himself up. His broad, slightly furred chest. The firm abs. His well-hung cock.

In fact, Nick had stood there the entire time, up until the shower turned off again. Just before Martin had opened the bathroom door, he'd sat back down at the table and opened his laptop, pretending he was engrossed in something. It was a good thing Martin had gone straight to his room instead of peeking over Nick's shoulder. He would have seen Nick was blankly staring at a pop-up ad for outdoor lawn furniture. He didn't have a lawn, or a house, for that matter.

Getting ready for bed officially stalled out on the cabin's equator, the center line between the too-short couch and the too-comfortable bed. The bed that had Martin in it.

Martin continued, "If you're worried that I regret last night, or that it was a one-off, rest assured I have no remorse for anything we did. And I hope I've made it clear that, for some unfathomable reason, I find both your body and your brain attractive." He paused. "Maybe the heart attack gave me brain damage, although my doctor never said anything."

"Fucker," Nick grumbled. His body made the decision for him and his feet moved toward the bedroom instead of the floor.

"I would be if you would get your sexy ass in here."

Nick's heart was racing as he stepped into the bedroom. Martin was waiting for him, propped up against the headboard with a cocky grin plastered his face—the rest of him naked. Desire flooded Nick's system, propelling him forward.

Martin Purdy was everything he'd ever fantasized about and more.

"Take those clothes off," Martin ordered. Nodding stupidly, Nick stepped closer to the bed and tugged off the shirt and briefs he'd changed into only minutes before.

Reaching out, Martin took his hand, effortlessly pulling Nick onto the bed. "You are damn sexy," he murmured, his thick fingers tracing a delicate pattern over Nick's skin.

Nick lifted one hand, intending to caress Martin's chest, but with an easy movement, Martin flipped their positions so Nick lay under him. Their stiff cocks pressed together, neither willing nor able to hide their desire.

"This okay?"

Nick nodded.

Leaning in, Martin captured Nick's lips in a fierce kiss. Nick moaned, his body responding eagerly as Martin's tongue explored his mouth and Nick's demanded its own entrance. As they kissed, Nick's greedy hands roamed over Martin's back, tracing the hard planes and curves of muscles that rippled under his skin.

Rising to his elbows, Martin hovered over Nick for a moment. Moonlight coming in through the window changed intensity as a cloud scuttled across the sky, blocking its view. New shadows crept across the room as Martin trailed a line of butterfly kisses down Nick's throat. Stopping there at the hollow, Martin breathed in, as if he was trying to take all of Nick's scent inside him.

"That tickles," Nick protested.

"You smell incredible," Martin insisted.

Nick shook his head. "I smell like your soap."

"I guess I like the smell of *me* on *you*," Martin growled against his skin.

Nick's cock pulsed and throbbed at Martin's words. Possibly, he groaned as well, but he wasn't certain. Maybe it had been Martin he'd heard.

Nick definitely groaned as Martin continued his epically slow journey down Nick's body. Gently kissing, nibbling, and breathing Nick in as he went. It was everything Nick could do to stay still and allow Martin to explore him. His fingers clutched at the bottom sheet, and he hoped not to put a hole in them.

"Fucking hell," Nick croaked, his patience failing him. "Is this what they call glacial speed?"

Looking up, Martin smiled. "I can go slower, if you like. I'm a geologist, after all."

"No," Nick managed to gasp out.

After what felt like an eon, Martin finally reached Nick's cock. Gazing down his body, Nick was struck by just *everything*. How fucking everything Martin was, how Nick didn't hold a candle to him. The thought was almost enough for his erection to disappear, but Nick was fundamentally a selfish man and more than anything else in the world right now—even world peace—he wanted Martin to hurry up and fuck him.

"Fuck!" he yelled as Martin's lips wrapped around the tip of him. That evil tongue slowly traced a path around Nick's other head. *"Maaartiiiin."*

Martin may have laughed, Nick couldn't tell, but he definitely didn't go any faster. Martin sucked and Nick gasped and panted, his cock pulsing out precome like he had a surplus. As hard as he tried not to cram himself down Martin's throat, his hips pumped against his will.

"I'm gonna come. Get inside me already."

Martin pulled off and Nick's cock smacked against his stomach. "Only because you asked so nicely."

Leaning across, Martin grabbed the lube and a condom that Nick hadn't even noticed he'd already taken out and placed on the bedside table.

"Fuck nice."

"Nothing wrong with nice. If you give me half a chance, I'll change your mind."

Nick reached for the lube, but Martin just grinned and squeezed it onto his own fingers. "You just lay back and enjoy the ride."

Next thing, Martin's thick finger was massaging his hole. Nick had never really cared much for a crap ton of foreplay, but Martin? Well, Martin took it to another level. One that had Nick panting and begging and basically a complete lunatic by the time Martin rolled on the condom and was knocking at his door.

"Damn," Martin said with a sigh, "your ass is incredible."

"Just incredible?" Nick said after getting his breath back. "I'll have you know—" Martin pressed past the first ring of muscle and Nick forgot whatever he'd been about to say.

Then Martin's cock found his prostate and Nick couldn't

think anymore. Nick raised one hand, intending to stroke himself, but Martin batted it away.

"I'll take care of you," he said as he pulled back and then pushed in again. Nick scrabbled at the sheet and squeezed his eyes shut, trying to both come and not come. He wanted it to be over because he was so hard it hurt. But he also didn't want it to end; he wanted to lie in Martin's bed and let him ravage him until there was nothing left.

They moved well together. There were no uncomfortable, awkward moments, the kind Nick regularly experienced when having sex, where he started second-guessing himself or his partner. Martin didn't allow second-guessing to begin. He just kept up his assault on Nick's prostate, dragging his cock back and forth, again and again across Nick's gland, until the only thing Nick thought he remembered was his name, and that was also in question.

Martin roared and arched his back, jamming his cock as far up Nick's ass as humanly possible. He was still pulsing into the condom, but he managed to wrap his large hand around Nick and started pumping him. Nick was so far gone that Martin's touch was all it took to send him over the edge. One, maybe one and a half pumps and Nick's entire body spasmed as the spark he'd been fighting off exploded into flame.

Clenching around Martin's softening erection, Nick dug his heels into the mattress as come shot from his dick and onto his stomach, long, ropey strands of it. He tried to open his eyes but truthfully, it was too much effort.

"Did I break you?" Martin asked with concern. Not much, just a tinge.

With difficulty, Nick peeled one eye open. "Good. I'm good."

"You're not arguing. Maybe I should call 9-1-1."

"Fuck off."

"Ah, that's much better."

Holding onto the condom, Martin pulled out of Nick's ass,

causing him to flinch. "Didn't hurt," he assured Martin. "Just weird, ya know."

Martin eyed him for a moment before getting up off the bed. "I'll take care of this and be right back." Seconds later, he returned with a warm cloth and gently wiped up Nick's abs. For Nick's part, he just lay there. He now knew exactly what a wet noodle felt like. If he tried to stand up, he suspected he'd just collapse onto the floor.

After returning the washrag to the bathroom, Martin slipped back into bed and pulled the covers over them both. Nick stayed on his back, his breathing slowing while he contemplated the ceiling.

Martin didn't say anything.

Did Nick want him to talk? He didn't know. Was he over-thinking? Why was he thinking at all? He'd just had the best sex of his life. Again. Was it possible to have the best twice?

With an irritated huff, Nick rolled onto his side and faced the bedroom door. He was drifting off when Martin set his warm, solid palm against Nick's back, almost as if he was keeping Nick from floating away.

It felt good. He was tempted to twitch it away but fell asleep before he could. His last conscious thought was, *What the fuck have I done now? And do I care?*

MARTIN

*Fact: The heaviest rocks in the world are made up of dense, metallic minerals. Two of the heaviest, or densest, rocks are **peridotite** or **gabbro**. Peridotite are the kind of rocks that naturally occurring diamonds are found in.*

The circus arrived in town a few days after the discovery. Martin didn't say circus, but he was thinking it. It was a smallish circus, comparatively. One instead of three rings. But it was, by definition, a damn circus. Dear had managed to keep the discovery quiet but obviously the news had gotten out. Martin suspected many folks in Cooper Springs would agree with him. He knew Nick did—all he'd had to do was glance over at him and note the disgusted expression on his face.

"What the actual fuck is that?" Nick grumbled, straightening to his full height and staring toward the police station. Their vantage from the rooftop gave them a bird's eye view.

An older Subaru wagon, and an even older Land Rover, had pulled up and parked directly in front of the station. A tall, dark-haired man got out of the first car and waited on the sidewalk while another dark-haired man and an equally tall woman climbed out of the Land Rover. Together, the three of them headed inside.

"Nothing we have to worry about. Let's just keep our noses out of police business," Martin replied innocently. As if that would happen.

Nick turned back to him, his expression outraged. "No offense to Chief Dear," he replied, his tone dripping with offense, "but he and Lani are the only two on the force with any brains. The folks that just arrived—they are the rest of the brains. I'm betting one of those people is Ethan Moore."

Martin nodded. They both felt a great responsibility toward the skull that Nick had discovered. It had revealed itself to them. *If* they hadn't chosen to go for a hike that day, it possibly would have never been found. Animals could have made off with it. Someone less scrupulous than they might have taken it as a souvenir. So many possibilities. But he and Nick were the ones who had found it and it felt—*momentous*.

"I tend to agree, but we need to focus on the work at hand, grasshopper. Hand me that stack of shingles. We have a job to finish up."

All the cabin roofs were just about done, which was excellent since the weather was only supposed to hold through the weekend. Then the rain would return. Luckily, they would be working inside the cabins after this: refinishing floors, repainting rooms, replacing windows, and more. A whole lot of things that started with *re*.

"Fine," Nick muttered in a way that indicated no such thing. But he hefted the stack of shingles closer to where Martin was finishing up.

"It is fine. We can head over to the Donkey in a bit and catch up on what we're missing out on."

"That's not the incentive you think it is." Nick watched him, a distinctly lascivious glint in his eye. "You made us get out of bed this morning."

"Mm-hmm," he agreed, pushing up the sleeves of the thick t-shirt he wore. "I did. I don't like to be rushed." Nick had tried to start something, but Martin had put the brakes on, much to Nick's obvious disgust. He hadn't wanted to be buried in Nick's ass and have the construction guys knocking at the door. "We'll probably have to shower before we head over."

Nick grumbled something that Martin thought was approval, although it was hard to tell with him sometimes. It was fine. He'd figure it out.

Picking up his roofing hammer again, Martin felt himself smiling. Who would have predicted *this*? Out with his stodgy, boring life—where he'd basically been waiting to retire and sit around until he died—and in with the new *risk-taking Martin*, the guy who'd left everything behind for a new life. The guy who'd offered a complete stranger a place to live and leveled it up to something a bit more. Something without a label, and that was just fine with him. He didn't need a label to be happy.

He was very happy in this future. Except for the murder. Except for Lizzy. Except for the skull of unknown origin. And the SUV Nick had seen, he added to himself.

It bothered him that they hadn't caught up with it that day they'd gone to the grocery store. The car had disappeared some-where in Aberdeen or along the way to Cooper Springs. Martin had especially hated that Nick had been reluctant to tell him about his suspicions because others had dismissed his concerns.

Sweat dripped into his eye, distracting him from his thoughts. Roofing was hard work. His gym-built muscles were feeling it. Swiping the sweat off his forehead, he glanced over to where Nick had his back to him, working just a few feet away.

Yeah, Martin didn't have a label for what was happening between the two of them, and that was just fine. He had no problem taking things as they came. There was no hurry, no need to rush anything.

From where they were occupied with putting the finishing touches on the second to last cabin roof, they had a front-row seat to the arrival of the news vans. The second circus ring.

"What the fuck is this now?" Nick said.

Martin assumed that was a rhetorical question because the lettering on the side of the van made it clear it was from a news station. Tucking his hammer into his tool belt, Martin straightened up and peered toward the police station before answering the question anyway. "That looks to be the news."

"The news," Nick spat out, as if saying a dirty word.

"It was bound to get out. And besides, someone is missing a loved one," he reasoned. "With any luck, someone will see the report and come forward."

Cooper Springs had started its reeling with Lizzy Harlow's murder, and CSPD still had no leads on that one. With the discovery of the skull, and the continued missing status of Blair Cruz, gossips had to be whispering the words *serial killer*. Martin himself hadn't heard anyone saying it yet, but they were. The situation had to have Chief Dear on edge.

"These folks aren't reporting news, they're looking to sensationalize something terrible and make money off it," Nick said bitterly.

As jaded as his opinion was, Martin agreed. Together they watched as the team, a reporter and a camera operator, emerged from the van. As they approached the front door of the police station, two things happened; another news van pulled up behind the first one and Chief Dear stepped out of the building. Of course, he and Nick couldn't hear what was being said from their vantage point, but Dear's body language was loud and clear: *Fuck off*. Martin wondered if maybe the mayor was a better choice for a press conference.

"Ho, boy, he looks pissed," Nick observed with glee.

Dear did indeed look pissed. After making his point, Dear swiveled and stormed into the building. His departure didn't cause the reporters to pack up and head back to wherever they'd come from. Instead, they began setting up on either side of the front steps, clearly planning to do their broadcasts from there.

"I wish I knew what they were saying," Martin said.

"We know what they're saying. 'Blah blah blah, serial killer on the loose, blah blah.' And that's all anyone is going to hear."

The CSPD entrance opened again, and one of the earlier arrivals emerged and began speaking to the waiting newscasters. Martin squinted, as if that would help bring the faraway figure into focus. It didn't.

"We could just go find out what's going on," Nick pointed out. "Click and Clack can finish up. They're getting paid after all."

Martin snorted, and absolutely did not glance over at the two guys from the town of Hoodsport that he'd hired to help him with the remodel. They seemed to know what they were doing, which was the point of hiring them. They were also Star Wars, Star Trek, and Stargate nerds who spent most of the time arguing the finer nuances of each world as they worked. *Fantasy worlds*, Martin wanted to point out to them. But they worked while they argued, so Martin had held his tongue.

"Better yet," Nick continued, "we could head over to the pub *now*—and save the shower for later—because I guarantee you Rufus is already in the loop, and we can kill two birds with one stone."

"How are we killing two birds?" Martin wanted to know.

"I'm hungry."

"There's food at home." As soon as his lips closed after the word *home*, Martin winced. "At the cabin," he corrected himself, but Nick didn't seem to notice.

"Yeah, but Magnus makes great black bean soup. But don't tell him I said so, or his head might explode."

"Did you…" Martin cocked his head and squinted at Nick. "Did you just make a joke?"

Scowling, Nick elbowed Martin. "I have a sense of humor." The pointy elbow pushed Martin off-balance. He teetered, and although they were only fifteen feet off the ground, his life still flashed before his eyes.

"Shit!" Nick grabbed his arm, steadying him. "I'm sorry!"

"I'd say the jury's out on the humor thing. But it's a *yes* on murderous tendencies," Martin grumbled as he made his way over to the ladder they'd set up on the backside of the small building. "Alright, I give in. Let's get cleaned up and head over to the Donkey. You're buying since you tried to kill me."

"It was an accident," Nick protested, clambering down the ladder and jumping to the ground instead of taking the last three rungs.

Martin did not jump, but carefully stepped off the last rung to the grass. There weren't many times when he felt all of his forty-four years, but this was one of them.

They pushed their way inside the pub, immediately spotting Rufus at the end of the bar holding court. He was surrounded by several people Martin didn't recognize, as well as Forrest Cooper and Dante Brown. Martin still hadn't forgiven Brown for his shitty comments the day they'd discovered the skull.

Magnus was there, of course. And Nick's friend, Liam, who smiled when he saw them come in together, but then he always seemed to be smiling. Another guy stood next to Liam, and Martin thought he ran the auto shop.

Martin had planned to have Nick take the lead on mining for information. But on second thought, *no*, bad idea. Martin shook his head at himself. Nick could end up doing more antagonizing than information-gathering. Mostly, Martin wanted to know who the guy was that had come out to talk to the reporters after Andre Dear had stormed back inside the station.

"Martin, Nick," Magnus called out when he saw them. "Make yourselves comfortable. Beer? Food? Both?"

"Both," Martin agreed. "Roofing is hard work."

"Looks like you're about done?"

Nick claimed the spot next to Liam, banging his friend on the shoulder with his fist. Sitting down on the other side of Nick, Martin nodded. "Yep. We can get started on the insides. I have the feeling roofing may have been the easy part."

Magnus laughed and, like any good publican, swiped at the already spotless bar in front of Martin and Nick with a damp towel.

Martin cocked his head toward Rufus. "What's the news?"

Magnus didn't have to look at his dad to answer. "That forensics gig the mayor hired showed up. Seems like we're finally going to get some answers around here."

"We saw a couple of news vans too," Nick said.

"Aye," Magnus agreed. "There's a big motherfucker dealing with them, I heard. They'll be running away with their tails between their legs soon enough. What can I get you two?"

While the publican took their food orders and poured pints, Martin listened to the conversation flowing around him. More folks were arriving too; the news had spread like wildfire.

"Anyone sitting here?"

Martin shifted to see an unfamiliar man with a hesitant expression on his face.

"Nope, it's all yours."

The stranger was in his late thirties or early forties. Unlike Martin, who'd gone silver by thirty-nine, the stranger's wavy, shoulder-length hair was still dark brown, just a few grays showing at his temples. Martin wondered if he just happened to be passing through or if he'd been drawn by the recent discoveries.

Once he was situated on the barstool, Martin held out his hand. "Martin Purdy."

He shook Martin's hand. "Nero Vik." He looked across at the taps. "What's good here?"

"Everything so far."

"Cool, cool." He nodded.

Magnus set Martin's beer and Nick's cider on the bar and turned his attention to the new newcomer. Martin kept his smile to himself, but he was glad someone else had the publican's attention for a minute.

On Martin's other side, Nick was in some sort of heated-yet-quiet discussion with Liam. He couldn't hear what they were talking about, so he sipped at his beer and let the chatter flow around him, waiting for the information he wanted to bob to the surface.

Nick's thigh bumped against his. It was a casual touch that Martin didn't think Nick was aware of. Martin liked it. A lot. It pleased him on a visceral level. Nick, consciously or not, was lowering his defenses around him. Last night—Martin smiled—last night had been incredible. He hadn't been sure Nick would join him in bed, but he had, and the result had been exactly what Martin wanted. And what Nick needed too, although he'd probably go to his deathbed before admitting as much.

"—and Martin here is the new owner."

"Sorry?" Martin dragged his attention away from memories of a naked, sweaty, panting Nick to the present.

"Oh." Nero smiled awkwardly. "I was asking about the cabins. Um, are any available to rent?"

"Not yet." Cabin Five—Nick's cabin—was basically ready apart from a few amenities. But that was Nick's spot. And the thought of waking up without Nick in his bed made Martin's stomach twist. He ignored it. "But I'm hoping to be up and going by late spring."

Nero was obviously disappointed by his response. "Dang.

I'm hoping to find something I can rent short term, but not just a weekend or a couple weeks. There doesn't seem to be a lot available." He smiled wanly. "Or anything, really."

"Why can't he rent Nick's place?" Magnus butted in. "He's not using it."

"What about me?" Nick asked, distracted from his conversation with Liam.

"This gentleman is looking for a rental," Magnus informed him. "Since you're shacked up with Martin these days, he could rent Five. That way Martin would be bringing in some cash instead of the other way around. As a businessman myself, I understand cash flow."

"I'm not—we're not—" Nick sputtered. "Just staying while" —he waved a hand—"it's being repaired."

"Is the roof not on? Is the electric working? The walls secure?" Magnus asked.

"Well—er, I guess," Nick responded like he'd only just realized that *his* cabin was, in fact, livable. Not perfect, but livable.

"So," Magnus continued, "what's to stop Martin from letting this fine fellow pay actual money to live in Five while the rest are finished? Then, when he's ready to hightail it out of here, you and Martin can finish it up."

Nick's mouth opened and closed several times. He stared at Martin. Martin shrugged. He felt slightly evil for letting Magnus keep talking without jumping in to protest. But honestly, he didn't see anything wrong with Magnus's suggestion. Nothing at all.

Nick eyed him intently. Was he waiting for Martin to say something? Maybe to protest that the situation was inconvenient? On his other side, Liam caught Martin's gaze. Nodding, he shot Martin a wink.

"It would be nice to have some income," Martin finally said. As if he'd actually been worried about money. "It's been all out-go for a while."

Which, of course, he'd planned for. But it was technically the truth.

"See? It's all settled," Magnus proclaimed, flipping the bar rag over his shoulder like he was refereeing a game. "Nick, you'll keep on with Martin, and Nero here has a place to stay. Done and done."

"Nero may want to see it first," Martin suggested calmly. "And Nick and I should talk too."

Magnus's bushy eyebrows drew together. "What's there to talk about? This is the perfect setup, win-win. We all want the resort to be successful, don't we?"

Nick's mouth opened, closed, and opened again. *Fish out of water.*

"Don't forget to breathe," Martin murmured, encouraging him with the nudge of an elbow. Martin *didn't*, however, contradict Magnus's edict that Nero showing up and needing a place to stay was a good situation all around.

He and Nick had been ignoring the fact that Nick could've already moved back into Cabin Five. Yes, the counters still needed to be replaced, but Click, or possibly Clack, had installed the new cabinets a few days ago along with the new windows. The water was hooked up and the electric as well. It wasn't perfect, but it would do.

"See?" Magnus continued. "Nico here isn't arguing with me —which is some kind of miracle. He's happy shacking up with Martin. I've seen him smile two whole times just this week."

NICK

Fact: About 70% of Earth's surface is covered by water. And, the coastal areas, which form the interface between land and water, are the site of geomorphic change. The movement of waves and tides, and the dissipation of large amounts of energy often causes rapid and spectacular changes in landforms along coastal areas.

What the fuck just happened?

Nick stared at Martin. Martin gazed back at him, the fucking picture of innocence. Nick shifted in his seat, wanting very much to argue, but—there was no argument. Aside from the fact that he was, if not happy these days, at least… content. As content as he'd ever been.

But he couldn't just accept that the feeling would last. Things didn't last for him. A bubble of panic tried to make its way to the surface.

He turned back to Liam. "Maybe I can—"

"Nope. Sorry, dude." Liam was shaking his head. "No can do. The moms are coming for a visit. Staying maybe a month, they're not sure yet."

"But." Nick sputtered again. "There's no room for them?"

Liam's house was hardly bigger than Martin's place and hadn't fit Nick at Thanksgiving. The spare bedroom looked like something out of one of those hoarding shows. Nick opened his mouth to point that out, but Liam got there first.

"Silas helped me clean out the junk room and Rufus rented me one of his trailers."

"But..." he let the word trail off. Still no argument. The bubble of panic had fizzled away.

"Let's have dinner while they're here. Not at my place," Liam qualified. "Here or at Pizza Mart. Somewhere, anyway."

"How did I not know they were coming?"

"I guess you've been a little distracted." Liam waggled his eyebrows. "I haven't seen much of you lately. You look good, Nick, happy." He poked Nick in the ribs. "Well, as happy as you've looked in a long time."

A hand landed on his thigh, grounding him. Nick didn't have to look down to know it was Martin's. He liked it there, he liked that Martin's touch calmed him. He didn't need a lot of fancy words. Fucking hell.

Martin leaned in to speak quietly. His lips brushed against the shell of Nick's ear, sending a jolt of lust directly to his cock. "You can stay with me as long as you want. I like having you around."

Nick opened his mouth to retort with something pithy like, *You're the only one,* but Martin squeezed his thigh—hard—and Nick snapped his lips shut. As if they were starring in some stupid Hallmark movie, sounds seemed to fade away. It was just the two of them.

The only person Nick was aware of was Martin. His hand on Nick's thigh, the weight of it, the promise. *Fucking, fucking hell.* He'd let himself fall in love with Martin Purdy. Staring into Martin's eyes, Nick waited for the panic to reappear. He needed to be panicking, he should be running fast and far. He *couldn't* love anyone. Love was a most dangerous emotion.

There was no panic.

This wouldn't last. It couldn't. Right? Martin squeezed his thigh again, a bit softer this time, and winked. "Whatever happens, it's all good."

How did Martin know the words that would keep Nick sitting right where he was instead of panicking?

"Here's that soup, Nico," Magnus said, setting the bowl down in front of him. "And the grilled cheese and onion for you, Martin. So," he said with an over-the-top smile, "are you taking Nero in?"

Kitten perched on the front windowsill, watching Martin and Nick approach. She was a smart little thing. When they got to the door, she jumped down, and they were greeted with meows that were too loud for her tiny body.

"Somebody's hungry," Martin commented as Kitten waltzed across to her empty food dish. "How about you take care of her highness and I'll find the keys so we can move one of the beds into Five?"

The new mattresses and bed frames had arrived the week before and for the time being were stored in Cabins Two and Three.

"Jane."

"What?"

"Jane. Her name is Jane."

Martin eyed him. "Why Jane?"

"Jane Doe is her full name, but Jane for short."

"I like it. Look," Martin began, "Nero will be here tomorrow and we need to get the cabin set up. We don't have time for all I want to do right now."

"Does part of that involve a shower?" Nick asked.

"Yes," Martin smiled wickedly, "but that part of the evening will have to wait. I feel a tiniest bit bad about letting Magnus steamroll you back there." He shrugged. "I do like having you here." He stepped closer. "I like being with you, Nick. I like *you*."

Nick frowned. He needed to tell Martin how wrong he was, that Nick was a bad bet.

"Ah, ah. Nope." Martin lay his index finger across Nick's lips. "I like you, Nick, as you are. I like the grouchy, argumentative bits and the less obvious bit that rescued a kitten. I like that brain of yours, how you think and solve problems. How much you care even if you try to hide it."

"You like my cock," Nick said, arching against him, unable to stand the compliments any longer.

"Yes, Nick, your cock and the rest of you. Just as you are." Martin grasped Nick's hips, holding him captive. "My cock definitely likes your cock." He looked over Nick's shoulder. "But right now, company is arriving soon, and"—giving Nick's hip one last squeeze—"I just needed to make sure you understand that being with you isn't a hardship. It isn't something I'm enduring. It's something I want."

He kissed Nick then. It wasn't a generic peck. It was a full-on soul-claiming kiss that left Nick breathless and hard.

When he could breathe again, Nick stepped back so he could adjust himself. "You're sure you don't have a brain injury? Old age, maybe?"

If he'd meant to insult Martin, it didn't work. Martin just laughed and kissed Nick again.

"For one, I'm not that much older than you, and for two, you make me feel younger than I have in years. Before you, before Cooper Springs, I was just existing. Now I'm living."

"I'm a moody fucker," he reminded Martin.

Martin widened his eyes in mock surprise. "No? Really?"

"Fuck off," Nick retorted, but he meant it in an almost loving way

Jane, tired of waiting for stupid humans to get a hint, started yowling louder. "For the love of Christ, cat, we're having a moment here. I'm coming."

"I don't like him," Nick said much later, after they'd moved the bedding and other stuff into Five—even though Nero Vik wasn't arriving until tomorrow. After their shower in the still-too-small shower stall. After they were in bed with the covers pulled over them again, and Jane was curled up at their feet.

"You don't like anyone, Nick," Martin said, his voice muffled by his pillow. He had one arm wrapped around Nick, spooning him. Keeping him close. Nick liked it.

"He's shifty," Nick insisted. "What's he doing here, in town? He's after something." Nick didn't know that for certain, but he had a feeling, a gut instinct. Something about this guy rubbed him the wrong way.

"He's fine, Nick. He's just a guy, and no doubt we'll get to know him while he's in town. Maybe he's down on his luck?" Martin pulled Nick even closer. "Maybe he's just a little lost and stopping for a while will give him that chance?"

"Maybe he's a rando serial killer. Seriously, I want to know, why is he here? In January? Who comes to Cooper Springs in January?"

"Didn't I hear that Liam's moms are visiting?" Martin pointed out.

"That's different. They used to live here, they know what it's like."

Martin snorted, and it tickled the back of Nick's neck. "Go to sleep. Tomorrow will be here sooner than we like. I've got a long list for you."

Nick started to insist he wasn't sleepy, but a massive yawn

betrayed him. "Fine, but I'm running a background check on him tomorrow. What kind of name is Nero Vik anyway? He should be easy enough to find."

"If that's what you need to do," Martin said, his voice slurry.

Pleased, Nick shut his eyes, knowing it would take forever to get to sleep. First thing tomorrow, he would check out Nero Vik.

"Ready for coffee, Sleeping Beauty?"

Nick dragged one eye open; he'd slept through the night—again. He almost felt human.

Wearing only a pair of cotton boxer briefs, Martin stood in the doorway smiling at him. Nick's foolish heart beat faster.

"Did I tell you Liam is carving a bunch of male princesses?" he asked. Martin wasn't a princess—although Nick thought Liam's princesses were sexy and beautiful—but Martin was a king.

"No," Martin said, moving to stand next to the bed. "Are they better than your dicks?"

Rolling his eyes, Nick arched his back and kicked the covers off, trying to get a rise out of Martin. "My dicks—all of them—are works of art."

He'd dropped the ball on the dick carvings, busy with other things recently. He'd bang out a few this week just to keep his hand in.

"Not arguing," Martin said, watching Nick's cock swell.

Wrapping his fingers around his erection, Nick first squeezed and then caressed himself, running his fingertips up and back down his length. His dick hardened further and his balls too.

Martin appeared mesmerized, his gaze molten. *Wanting.* The bulge in his boxers growing as Nick watched. He wanted Nick and it blew Nick's mind.

Shaking his head as if he really had been hypnotized, Martin quickly stripped off his briefs and tossed them aside. His cock was thick and long, just like he was. It bobbed as he moved, swinging Nick's direction. As he watched, a droplet of precome oozed from the tip, sending a throb of desperate need down his spine.

"I'm not quite ready for coffee yet," Nick said, his voice hoarse, "but I'm ready for you."

"Where is he?" Nick growled. They'd cleaned up, had coffee and bagels, and finished organizing Cabin Five. It was noon now and Nick was feeling impatient. Martin had texted Nero Vik a half hour ago telling him the cabin was ready, but he hadn't answered.

Nick was standing at the window, arms crossed over his chest, frowning at the forest on the other side of town while also watching the misty rain float down from the heavy clouds over Cooper Springs—as if Vik might just appear out of nowhere somehow. Jane perched on his shoulder like a tiny gargoyle, also peering out the window.

"Somebody forgot to tell Vik that cell coverage in the area was random," Martin said from where he was sitting on the couch, "or his phone is dead."

Or the creep knew Nick was on to him and had changed his mind about staying with them. Maybe he'd given Martin a fake number.

"It's not a big deal, Nico," Martin said, as if he knew exactly where Nick's thoughts were headed. "We'll just head over to the pub and see if he's around and if he's not, we can leave a message for him there. Probably he went into Aberdeen or something—we don't know where he's been staying—and we'll see him when he gets back."

All true facts, and yet, also irritating.

"So logical. You always have an explanation."

Martin came to stand next to him. "Most of the time, solutions are simple. You, Nick, like things to be convoluted and complicated—I like that about you, a lot."

Nick started to protest—mostly because, even if he refused to admit it out loud, praise from Martin made Nick's stomach do a pleased little twist—but just at that moment, a black SUV careened into view.

"Do you see that?" Nick exclaimed, jabbing his finger at the glass. Jane hissed and jumped down, stalking away in a huff, her fur standing on end. Pretty much exactly how Nick felt.

"Is that it?" Martin asked, his voice rising as he leaned toward the window. "Is that *the* SUV?"

"I'm sure of it," Nick said grimly. "Driving too fast and I'll bet it's going to head into the back of town in a minute."

Martin grabbed his car keys off the mantle. "Let's go, see if we can catch up with it."

A minute later, Martin was behind the wheel and Nick was strapped into the passenger seat. Gunning the engine so gravel sprayed behind them, he pulled out of their drive and headed the same direction as the black SUV.

"There it goes," Nick said unnecessarily. "Don't lose it."

"Don't you worry, Starsky, I've got this."

"Starsky, my ass. You just keep your eyes on the road."

Just as Nick predicted, the SUV turned just past the Pizza Mart. Martin stepped on the gas and they careened around the corner seconds later. Thank fuck, there were no other cars on the road, although Nick had spotted Wanda Stone unlocking the thrift shop while Rufus Ferguson looked on. Rufus frowned at Martin's car as they sped past.

Nick grabbed at the suicide handle. "Jesus Christ, Martin. My life flashed before my eyes. If Rufus recognized us, we're going to be on the receiving end of a traffic safety lecture."

Martin slowed a bit, but the other car was already a block ahead of them. Nick knew it was going to turn off again; this was another dead-end street. There wasn't anything at the end of this road other than homes and blackberry bushes. Probably a path to the high school, but the car wouldn't be able to take that.

"There it goes," Martin said grimly. He gripped the steering wheel so tightly his knuckles were white.

The black car turned again. For the life of him, Nick could not figure out where it was heading. Keeping his eyes pinned on the vehicle as if it might disappear in a cloud of smoke, Nick wondered if the driver knew they were being followed or if they were a habitual turn-indicator ignorer.

Just ahead of them, a silver sedan began inching out of a driveway. "Dammit." Martin was forced to slow to a crawl while Mr. Gaziano's car lurched into the street. The eighty-year-old finally passed them by with a smile and a wave. Two blocks ahead of them now, the other car turned again.

By the time they got to the corner, it was nowhere in sight.

"Dammit," Nick growled, "we were so close."

"Fucking hell." Martin banged the steering wheel in frustration. He drove slowly now so they could look down at every intersection. "Did you get a plate number?"

Nick grimaced at his stupidity. "I... forgot?" He'd been so intent on knowing where the car was going, he hadn't thought about getting the plate number. "It's not like the cops would look it up and just tell us whose car it is."

"What's down that way?" Martin asked, ignoring Nick's reply.

They were at the northeastern edge of town. Right or left were the only ways to go. One direction of the road eventually led to The Strip, the other to the forest.

"Pretty much just forest land. A few houses tucked away. There's a campground, but it's closed for the season."

"No chance of someone sneaking in and illegally camping?"

"I mean, I suppose so, but Critter and Mags take that shit seriously."

"Okay, okay. Fine." Martin banged the steering wheel again, more lightly this time. "Since we're close, let's stop in at the Donkey. Maybe Nero will be there, and we can get him sorted out."

Vik wasn't in sight when they walked in. The barstools they usually sat in were open, though. Wordlessly, Nick and Martin sat down, their shoulders brushing as they did so.

"Have you seen Nero Vik today?" Martin asked when Magnus stopped in front of them.

Magnus shook his head. "Nope. What can I get you guys? You look a little tense."

Martin quickly glanced at Nick. Nick shrugged; he wasn't going to say anything. He'd already been told he was imagining things.

"Nah," Martin replied as he shook his head, smiling back at Magnus, "but I could really use a pint of something tasty. If you see Vik, let him know the cabin's ready. We'll get his info from him and be good to go."

"What the actual fuck? Are you seeing what I'm seeing?" Nick demanded, repeatedly shutting his eyes and opening them again to make sure he wasn't hallucinating.

They'd had a beer each and shared an order of fries—thank fuck also that Martin did not like the heinous aioli Liam did because that could've been a deal breaker—and then headed back home.

"I'm seeing it," Martin confirmed.

A single car was parked in the lot below the cabins. A lone, very shiny, black Toyota Sequoia.

Martin pulled in and parked next to it. The driver's side door opened, and Nero Vik appeared, giving them a small wave.

"What the actual fuck," Nick said again.

Martin waved back and opened his door to climb out. "Come on."

Nick wasn't sure if he was glad Martin didn't say anything about Nick being a complete fool or if he was pissed because he should have.

"Sorry," Nero said as he tugged a ball cap over his head, presumably to keep the wind from having its way with his long hair. "I guess I was in a dead zone and didn't get your text till a few minutes ago. I drove right over." His glance bounced from Martin to Nick and back to Martin. "I hope that was okay?"

MARTIN

Fact: Thundereggs usually look like ordinary rocks on the outside, but slicing them in half and polishing them often reveals delicate patterns and colors.

Nick was flopped on the couch with one arm thrown over his face. Jane had immediately taken up residence on his chest.

"I'm an idiot," he announced for the umpteenth time since they'd given Nero the tour and the key to Five.

"It's a mistake anyone could make. You're not an idiot, Nick. You saw something out of the ordinary that bothered you. It turned out not to be what you thought, but that doesn't make you an idiot."

Martin pushed Nick's feet down so he could sit next to him. Jane shot him an evil look as she climbed up the cushions to her usual spot.

"I'd convinced myself that the car had something to do with Lizzy Harlow's death." Nick snorted. "Like we were going to make a citizen's arrest and end up the Hardy Boy Heroes of Cooper Springs. I hate that her body was just left there at the bridge and I heard nothing that night. It feels like I failed a test."

If Martin had learned anything about Nick Waugh in the past months, it was that he held himself to a standard that was almost impossible to reach.

"You didn't fail a test. There is no test when it comes to something like this. I want her killer brought to justice as much as you do. Besides, have you considered that Nero Vik doesn't own the only black Toyota Sequoia in the state? In the region? The one we saw today, we don't know if that was Nero's or someone else's. We didn't get a plate and"—he shrugged, leaning into Nick's warm body—"we just don't know."

"I don't like not knowing."

"I get that."

Nick abruptly changed the subject. "I've decided not to go back to the International Press."

"Okay." Nick had told Martin that his contact there kept emailing with offers and that even though he needed the money, he wasn't sure about accepting.

"I don't feel it anymore. It's not even that I ended up in the middle of a gunfight."

Jane chose that moment to tumble down from the top of the couch into Nick's lap. Almost automatically, he started to stroke her tummy, which earned him a four-legged hand grab and an attempted bite. Nick laughed, a sound Martin loved.

As tempted as he was, Martin kept his mouth shut. He knew Nick wanted to stay, but Nick needed to say it with his own words.

"I hate talking about this kind of stuff," Nick huffed, still focused on Jane. "Liam says I should try and express myself more. Like, about happy shit." He quickly glanced at Martin. "Happy is a weird space for me. But since we got together, I think I'm the closest I have been in a long time. I don't know how, or why, but…" he sighed as if resigned to a fate worse than death. "I like you a lot, Martin."

Martin laughed, then gently picked up Jane and set her on the floor before curling one hand behind Nick's neck and laying a claiming kiss on his lips. Nick moaned and shifted, wrapping his free arm around Martin's shoulders. The rapid pulse in Nick's throat, the way his scruff rasped against Martin's cheek, his short, spikey hair between Martin's fingers as they kissed. It was everything Martin'd ever dreamed of and an unfathomable more—it was love, he knew.

He pulled away. Nick stared up at him, his pupils blown and his lips puffy.

"I like you a lot too, Nick. Just the way you are. I'm glad you're not planning on traveling soon. But know that I would never stop you if that's what you wanted to do."

"But I don't have a job."

Martin traced a lazy line down Nick's strong jawline.

"We'll sort it out. Maybe your dicks will go viral, and tourists will flock to town."

Nick burst out laughing and pushed Martin off him.

"Those aren't dicks, asshole. They're mushrooms."

"Mushrooms?" Martin squinted as if he had one of the offending carvings in front of him to look at. "Wow. Okay, so maybe not a world-famous artist. Meh, that's okay."

"Fuck off," Nick said without heat.

"Fuck, yes. Off, no," Martin replied, waggling his eyebrows.

"I've created a monster," Nick mock-complained. "Don't we have work to do today?"

Martin's cell phone interrupted them, buzzing from where he'd dropped it on the mantle along with his car keys. Rising to his feet, he crossed the room to see who was calling.

"It's Simon," he told Nick. "I better answer, or he'll start going on about Sasquatch serial killers. Hello," Martin said as he started toward the kitchen, intending to make an espresso.

"Martin! It's Simon."

"Yes," Martin said dryly, "I suspected as much from the Caller ID."

"Cool, cool. How's it going? What are you up to today?"

It seemed like an innocent question, but there was something in his tone that had Martin's eyes narrowing.

"The usual," he said vaguely. "Why?"

"Road trip. Charley and I should be there in about half an hour, just dropping by."

"What? Why?" Martin demanded, pulling the phone away from his ear and staring at it. As if that would explain why Simon was calling to tell him they were "dropping by." He put the phone to his ear again. "Not that I'm not happy to see you, but please explain how you're *dropping by* when it's a two-hour drive?"

"Three-day weekend, baby," Simon crowed. "We're having the usual June weather in January, so it's perfect timing. It's been two months, and I want to see how you're doing in real life. These short and quick updates are just not doing it for me. Charley found some weird castle a little further south that he wants to check out, so we won't stay long."

Thank fuck for that. Martin sucked in a lungful of air as he stared at the cat clock, noting the time. He was not letting Simon come waltzing into town without telling him that he and Nick were a thing. Plus, he figured that Simon very much suspected something was going on between Nick and him, even if Martin hadn't said as much. Simon was not so much *dropping by* as *checking up*.

"Before you roll in here ready to rumble," Martin began, "I have something to tell you."

Nick pushed past Martin into the kitchen, leaning against the counter with his arms crossed.

"I'm not rumbling," Simon protested weakly.

"Nick and I are together," Martin informed Simon, holding Nick's stormy gaze with his own. "Nick is officially living here in the cabin with me."

"Together?" Simon sputtered. "Living together? How did that happen?"

Continuing to hold the phone to his ear, Martin closed in on Nick, pressing him back against the counter.

"You're a smart man, Simon. I think you know how."

"But… he was so rude."

"He had his reasons." Martin ground his hips against Nick, who rolled his eyes and let his arms drop. "And we've gotten to know each other. I like Nick, a lot, just how he is."

"Huh." There was muttering and then Simon was back. "Twenty minutes."

"Meet us at the pub."

For the second time that day, Martin and Nick walked into the Steam Donkey. He'd seen Simon's Jeep in the parking lot, so he knew Charlie and he had beaten them there.

"Over here," Simon called out, as if Martin wouldn't be able to find them. Nick hadn't wanted to come, but Martin had put his foot down *and* bribed him with a blow job. Orgasms definitely put Nick in a more mellow mood. Maybe he and Charley wouldn't kill each other. Miracles were known to happen.

They slid into the booth across from Simon and Charley.

"Nick, this is my ex-work husband Simon and his real husband, Charley. Guys, this is Nick."

Charley shot Martin an evil grin. "I told you all the boys would come running."

"Charley," Simon said warningly, putting his hand under the table.

Charley shifted, protesting, "I'm just pointing out that I was right. Martin is a catch."

"Anyway," Simon began, "like Martin said, we used to work together."

"I was Simon's emotional support while he pulled his head out of his ass and sorted everything out with Charley," Martin added. "Just in case these two yahoos make it sound like they are the epitome of how to start a relationship. We are miles ahead of them."

"Hey," Simon protested.

"He's not wrong," Charley said. "So, let's skip all that and get down to the good stuff." He pinned Nick with a stare. "How do I meet the guy who carves the princesses? Someone posted a picture of a couple of them on Insta and whoever the artist is, they're talented. Sorry, dude." Charley shook his head. "I've seen better dicks than yours drawn by six-year-olds, so I don't think it's you. Dicks just aren't that hard."

"Oh my god," Simon groaned, slapping his hand over his eyes.

Next to him, Nick angled forward and spoke quietly, like he was telling Charley a military secret. "They should be hard *all the time*. But"—he leaned back again—"if you must know, my friend Liam is the person who carved those."

"Can I meet him?" Charley asked. "And when?"

This time, when Simon and Charley drove away, Martin and Nick stood side by side, watching as their taillights disappeared around the bend.

"No offense—I ended up liking your friends—but I'm glad they're gone."

"My sentiments exactly. Ready to go home? Jane's probably pissed off."

"Jane is always pissed off."

They both looked toward the cabin. Jane sat on the windowsill, her mouth opening and closing as she complained.

"You should see if she'll take a leash. Maybe she'd like to be outside."

"Maybe," Nick said skeptically.

"I had a cat growing up that loved to hike with us," Martin told him. "We never put her on a leash. She hated the car but also wouldn't let us go away without her. Of course, that was in ancient times, but she'd hike right along with us and sleep in the tent too. Singed her butt a couple times at the fire pit. There's no more disgusting smell than burning cat hair."

"What happened to her?"

Martin was pretty sure Nick imagined Basty had been eaten by a bear or lost in the wilderness forever.

"To Basty? The meanest cat that ever lived? She died peacefully at twenty-six, while I was getting my PhD. Probably dreaming about the two—or was it three?—dogs she sent to the vets."

Nick stared at him. "Are you kidding me?"

"No, but the dogs were assholes, and she only weighed six pounds. Come on." Martin grabbed Nick's hand, weaving their fingers together. "Let's get inside and placate Jane so she doesn't kill us in our sleep."

Nick looked down at their joined hands and then back at Martin, a hint of a smile playing on his lips.

"Okay."

EPILOGUE - AUGUST

Fact: Gold is one of the most precious and disputed metals in the world. Scientists believe that 80% of the gold on earth has not yet been discovered.

"Where did you say we were going?" Martin asked again.

Nick was driving, and he glanced over before returning his attention to the road. "I didn't. That's the point of surprises."

"I don't like surprises."

"That's total crap," Nick scoffed. "You love surprises. Especially the naked kind."

"I do like those specific surprises," Martin conceded, continuing to ogle Nick's profile and wonder how on earth he'd ended up with Nick Waugh in his life.

It was a gorgeous midsummer evening, and the sun wasn't due to set for a couple of hours yet. They were driving south on Highway 101, having already passed through Aberdeen, and were now headed only Nick knew where.

"It's a surprise, and it's staying that way until we get there. Not much longer."

"Hmph." But Martin relaxed against the passenger seat, resigned to his fate. Nick was remarkably stubborn. He'd announced this morning that they had plans and nothing Martin had resorted to made Nick tell him what they were doing or where they were going.

While Nick drove, Martin took the opportunity to take in the beauty that was the northern Oregon coast. Soon enough, they'd be passing through Cannon Beach with its magnificent haystack rocks.

"Are we staying over somewhere?"

"Maybe."

They were, then; that was great. Martin found he enjoyed spying on what other small resorts and places like theirs offered.

Nick flicked the blinker, turning onto a side road.

"What is this?"

Nick slowed further and took a left into a driveway. A posted sign welcomed them to Norwegian Wood.

"Don't ask me why it's called that, I don't know," Nick said before Martin opened his mouth. They continued up the drive, eventually parking by an old barn and house that looked heavily repurposed. In the field next to the barn was a huge white canvas.

Not a canvas, Martin realized. It was a screen.

"Is this an outdoor movie theater?"

Nick grinned and nodded. "Yes, and the restaurant is supposed to be five stars. They serve mostly salmon and steak. We have reservations so we can eat before the movie."

"What movie?"

Nick's grin grew wider.

"*Tango and Cash*. The best buddy cop movie of all time."

Martin couldn't help but return his grin—even if he was wrong.

"There's a nine-hole golf course too. We could do something like that at home." Nick's eyes grew wide. "But what if we made it a kitschy putt-putt course with Sasquatches and Kraken? Something parents would think was fun too."

Nick climbed out of the car, pocketing the keys. "Did I tell you it's a double feature with *22 Jump Street?*"

Martin met Nick's excited gaze over the top of the car and saw he was still smiling. Who would've predicted this Nick Waugh was hidden underneath all the natural grumpiness? Mind, Martin was pretty much the only one who ever saw this side of Nick—and that was just fine with him.

"You seriously think *Tango and Cash* is better than *22 Jump Street?*"

"Better isn't a word that applies to these movies," Nick clarified. "It's a matter of nuance."

"Nuance, my ass."

Martin walked around to meet Nick in front of the car.

"I'll nuance your ass," Nick informed him, "but it will have to be after the movies. We need to get checked in and eat dinner before that. And *somebody* is going to have to be quieter than usual. We're sleeping in a yurt."

"Hey," Martin protested, "I'm quiet."

Grabbing his hand, Nick said, "I love you, babe, but you are not quiet."

Martin's healed and awakened heart pounded against his ribs. Nick had never said those words before. Martin believed Nick loved him, but hearing the words was different.

"I love you too, Nico."

Nick smiled and simply replied, "I know."

Next up is *Red Flagged!* Will they, or won't they? Police Chief Andre Dear and ex-undercover cop, Dante Brown go head-to-head in this heart pounding thriller. The two men have a history. Andre Dear thought he'd put an end to it. Dante Brown plans on changing his mind. But first they have a murder to solve. And when Dante's niece is in mortal danger the two men will have to find a way to get along.

Stay up to date on all things Elle related by joining the Highway to Elle. A weekly newsletter with all the Elle news you'll ever need!

A THANK YOU FROM ELLE

If you enjoyed *Below Grade*, I would greatly appreciate if you would let your friends know so they can experience Martin, Nick, and the rest of Cooper Springs As with all of my books, I have enabled lending on all platforms in which it is allowed to make it easy to share with a friend. If you leave a review for Below Grade or any of my books, on the site from which you purchased the book, Goodreads, Bookbub, or your own blog, I would love to read it! Email me the link at elle@ellekeaton.com

Keep up-to-date with new releases and sales, *The Highway to Elle* hits your in-box approximately every two weeks, sometimes more sometimes less. I include deals, freebies and new releases as well as a sort of rambling running commentary on what *this* author's life is like. I'd love to have you aboard! I also have a reader group called the Highway to Elle, come say hi!

ABOUT ELLE

Writing inclusive romance featuring complex characters and a unique sense of place is my happy place. The characters start out broken, and maybe they're still a tad banged up by the end, but they do find the other half of their hearts and ALWAYS get their happily ever after.

In 2017 I pressed the publish button for the first time and never looked back—making this the longest period of time I've stuck with a job--in my entire life. Currently, there are over thirty Elle Keaton books available for you to read or listen to.

I love cats and dogs. Star Wars and Star Trek. Pineapple on pizza, and have a cribbage habit my husband encourages. Connecting with readers is very important to me. If you are so inclined, join my newsletter, The Highway to Elle, and keep up to date with everything Elle related.

Including, but not limited to, 'where are my glasses?', and 'why are there cats?'. I can also be found on Facebook, Instagram and occasionally TikTok.

Copyright © 2023 by Elle Keaton

All rights reserved.

No part of this book may be reproduced in any form or by any electronic or mechanical means, including information storage and retrieval systems, without written permission from the author, except for the use of brief quotations in a book review.

Cover design T.E. Black Designs

Cover Image Furiousphotog

Cover Model Nathan Belanger-LeCloux

Edited by The Elusive SB

www.ingramcontent.com/pod-product-compliance
Lightning Source LLC
Chambersburg PA
CBHW061526310726
48972CB00008B/2343